THE CURSE OF THE WERE-HYENA

A Monstertown Mystery

THE CURSE OF THE WERE-HYENA

A Monstertown Mystery

by Bruce Hale

DISNEY • HYPERION

Los Angeles   New York

First Edition, July 2016
1 3 5 7 9 10 8 6 4 2
FAC-029191-16074
Printed in Malaysia

Library of Congress Cataloging-in-Publication Data
Hale, Bruce.
Curse of the were-hyena : a Monstertown mystery /
by Bruce Hale.—First edition.
pages cm
Summary: When Mr. Chu, the coolest teacher ever,
develops some very unusual habits and appears to be a
monster, best friends Carlos and Benny investigate.
ISBN 978-1-4847-1325-9
[1. Monsters—Fiction. 2. Teachers—Fiction. 3. Schools—Fiction.
4. Best friends—Fiction. 5. Friendship—Fiction. 6. Blessing and
cursing—Fiction. 7. Mystery and detective stories.] I. Title.
PZ7.H1295Cu 2016
[Fic]—dc23   2015010136

Reinforced binding
Visit www.DisneyBooks.com
[Sustainable logo/info]

To the kid at Pine Grove Elementary who said I should write a mystery involving monsters, and to the boys of El Camino Elementary who helped me with the hero

Thanks also to my beta readers, Arturo Vega and Raquel López

WHAT DO YOU do when your favorite teacher starts turning into a were-hyena? Flee in terror? Try to cure him? Bring him carrion snacks?

Forget about homework habits and curriculum goals—*this* is the kind of practical stuff they should cover at back-to-school orientation.

But they don't.

Maybe if they had, I wouldn't have found myself stuck up a tree with my best friend, Benny Brackman, scared out of my wits and smelling his funky feet.

"Did you *have* to kick your shoes off?" I asked, trying not to inhale through my nose. This was hard, since I was panting and his stinky feet were just above me.

"You know I climb better when my toes can grip," said Benny.

"Yeah? Well, climb higher!"

"I can't," he said. The narrow branch swayed under his weight.

I gripped it tighter. "If you don't, we'll be monster kibble."

"I bet it gave up." The whites of his eyes gleamed in the dimness. "Has it gone away yet?"

I glanced down. At the base of the oak tree, a half-human, half-hyena creature from my darkest nightmares paced in and out of the silver moonlight, snarling up at us. Its furry, ultrabuff body would've put a WWE wrestler's to shame. Its powerful jaws looked as if they could snap your neck like a carrot stick.

"Still there," I said. "And it's not a happy monster."

"Don't worry, Carlos," said Benny. "Everyone knows dumb old were-hyenas can't climb trees."

At this, the monster cocked its shaggy head and growled. Its red-rimmed eyes narrowed.

"Benny!"

"What?"

"*A*, don't insult something that's trying to eat you . . ." I said.

Sizing up our tree, the hyena-man took a few steps back.

"Why not?" said Benny.

"It only makes it try harder," I said. "And *B*—"

In a rush, the were-hyena launched itself at the tree trunk, scrabbling with claws like hooked daggers.

I gulped. "—and *B*, why *wouldn't* it be able to climb? Bears can climb."

And sure enough, those sharp claws sank into the bark, and the monster hauled itself higher up the trunk.

Benny's eyes popped. "That's not fair!" he cried. "In all the wolfman movies we've watched, have you *ever* seen a werewolf climb a tree?"

"Never," I said. "But, Benny?"

"Yeah?"

"This isn't a werewolf. And this isn't a movie."

Time out. I know, things are just getting interesting, but I'm being a bad narrator.

I started our story at an exciting part, like our teacher says we should, but I just realized you have no idea who we are or how we came to get treed by a were-hyena. (Not that we actually *came* there to get treed by a were-hyena, but you know what I mean.)

Let's back up to the day when everything changed. The day when we realized our town was misnamed—that instead of Monterrosa, it should be called Monstertown.

I'll start with the day the monster movies became *real*.

Chapter One

Freaky-Deaky Teacher

MONSTERS ARE all around us. The thing under the bed that kept you up, spooked and sleepless, in first grade? Totally real. The creature in the lake that your parents called a figment of your imagination? Real, too.

Just because you haven't seen them—*yet*—doesn't mean they're not there.

Now, I'm the first to admit it: I read lots of books, watch lots of movies, and have an overactive imagination. Yes, I once ran screaming from a museum when I thought I saw a suit of armor twitch. And yes, I had to sleep with all my lights on and a speargun beside me for a week after I saw that shark movie.

But my actual life has officially gotten weirder than my imagination.

And that's saying something.

The change from normal to *loco* began on the day my teacher growled. But to really understand it, you have to understand my teacher.

Mr. Chu is the coolest teacher at Monterrosa Elementary—and I'm not just saying that in the usual my-teacher's-cooler-than-yours way. Everybody thinks so. I mean, sure, he teaches the same subjects as the other fourth-grade teachers, but the *way* he teaches leaves them all in the dust.

Like how he wore a toga and juggled olives for our unit on ancient Rome. Or how he helped us understand probability by charting how movie sequels nearly always stink like a dead rat in the attic. Or the time he demonstrated gravity by tossing a chair out a second-story window.

After Mr. Chu turned our classroom into a lab and had us figure out how much electricity it would take to bring Dr. Frankenstein's monster to life, all the kids at school wanted to be in our class.

Mr. Chu was short, stocky, and as bald as an NBA all-star (but without the muscles). He kept order in the classroom with a smile and a calm word, never losing his cool.

Until that dreadful day.

It was oral report time, otherwise known as cruel and unusual punishment. (Even with a great teacher, I'd rather eat live potato bugs than give an oral report. Come to think of it, *that* would make an awesome report.) Zizi Lee had just finished telling us everything that had gone wrong on her family's trip to China. She sat down.

Those of us who hadn't gone yet looked anywhere but at the teacher. I studied the corner of my desktop, where some poor kid long before me had carved BORN TO PUN.

Then I heard it:

"Carlos Rivera," Mr. Chu boomed in his game-show voice, "come on dowwwn!"

I gulped. Suddenly sweat gushed from my pores like a river and my throat went desert-dry. (Too bad this wasn't a science report; I had my own microclimate.)

Picking up my shoe box, I shuffled to the front of the room. My buddy Benny Brackman gave me a thumbs-up. His blue eyes sparkled under his mop of curly hair, and he seemed as enthusiastic about my report as he was about anything that caught his fancy. (Or maybe he was just happy he'd already had his turn.)

From two rows over, Tyler Spork made a *pfft* sound of disgust. His sidekick, Big Pete, snickered.

I tried to ignore Tyler, who was winning the competition for Biggest Jerk in Room Thirteen by a landslide. Setting my box on the edge of Mr. Chu's desk, I wiped my palms on my jeans and faced the class.

"Um," I began. Twenty-six faces stared at me. "I, uh . . ."

Sheer brilliance so far. Obviously, public speaking was a

breeze—like tap-dancing on a tiny log as it shot down the rapids.

"Fascinating," cooed Tyler. "Do go on."

My face went hot.

Several girls shushed him. I glanced at Mr. Chu, who was frowning into space, head tilted, a million miles away.

I cleared my throat. "My, uh, report is about my dog, Zeppo."

The teacher made a face as if he smelled something bad. A few kids chuckled.

Reaching into the box, I found a photo and held it up. "Zeppo is a dachshund-Labrador-poodle mix. We call him a doxadoodle."

Tyler yawned, but some of the girls went *awww*, like girls do.

I pressed onward. "The, uh, thing that makes me crazy about Zeppo is that he'll chew *anything*." (Our oral report theme was Something That Makes Me Crazy. I told you Mr. Chu was cool.)

Putting away the picture, I lifted something else out of the box. "Exhibit A: my undies."

This got a huge *ewww!* from the class. Benny grinned widely. I glanced back at our teacher and noticed him leaning toward the box, sniffing, with this weird look on his face.

"Um, as you can see, Zeppo chewed up almost everything but the waistband. But that's not all. . . ." I replaced

the no-longer-tighty-whities and pulled out a mangled plastic tube. "Exhibit B: our vacuum cleaner. And he didn't just chomp on this hose—he got the bag and cord, too."

Tyler leaned across the aisle toward Big Pete and stage-whispered, "What a dweezle. Too bad the dog didn't chew up his report."

More chuckles from the class. More blushing from me.

Normally Mr. Chu has a zero-tolerance policy for rudeness. I turned to see why he hadn't said anything, but he hadn't even noticed Tyler's comment. Our teacher was laser-focused, his nose right over my shoe box. In fact, Mr.

Chu didn't even blink when I returned the hose and fished out a second photo.

What was up with him?

"Exhibit, um, C," I said, showing the picture around. "The wall. Yup, my dog actually chewed on the wall."

But as I reached for my final item, the mauled tennis shoe, Mr. Chu surprised me. He peeled back his lips and growled—a serious growl, like a Doberman giving one last warning before taking off your arm. His eyes rolled upward, showing only the whites, which totally creeped me out.

All the little hairs on my body stood straight up. It felt like someone had dumped a six-gallon slushie down my back.

Stepping away, I squeezed out a nervous laugh. "Uh, very funny, Mr. Chu. Nice dog impression."

My teacher kept snarling at the box, like he hadn't even heard me.

"Mr. Chu?" I said.

Finally, he blinked and shook his head. "Mmm? Oh. Fabulous report, Carlos. Let's hear it, everyone."

My classmates clapped, but with some confusion. I hadn't finished yet. But now, apparently, I had.

Collecting my shoe box, I mumbled a thank-you to Mr. Chu.

He sniffed again, glowered, and muttered, "Dogs," the way you'd say "cauliflower" if it turned up in your ice cream sundae. Then he scratched at his bandaged hand, which he'd told us came from a "bite from a strange-looking dog" when he was walking past the graveyard last night.

Call it a wild hunch, but something told me our teacher didn't much care for man's best friend.

I shuffled back to my desk and stowed my shoe box.

From the next row, Benny caught my eye. *Weirdness*, he mouthed.

"Weirdness," I agreed.

But the weirdness was only just beginning.

As we returned from recess, I passed behind Mr. Chu's desk, where he sat grading homework. What I saw made me stumble over my own feet: on his cueball-smooth head, a tiny forest of short, dark hairs had sprouted.

Since earlier that morning.

And not just behind the ears where he still had a little hair left, but all over.

Benny noticed it, too. "Wow, Mr. C! Your hair's really coming back."

Our teacher lifted a hand and ran it over his scalp. "I'll be darned," he said. "I guess that emu oil must be doing the trick."

"Uh, yeah," I said.

At that, an odd light came into Mr. Chu's eyes. He gave a high-pitched giggle that lasted an uncomfortably long time—long enough that other kids returning from recess shied away.

I looked over at Benny. "Guess he's *really* happy to have hair again," I said as we returned to our seats.

Our math lesson started out all right—with a scavenger hunt to see how many geometric shapes we could find in the classroom. We all spread out, searching high and low, recording what we spotted.

I'd already found a circle (Mr. Chu's coffee mug), a triangle (Amrita's notebook, from above), and a square (Tyler Spork's head). I was searching for some good parallel lines, when—

"Whoa!"

I turned. Last time I looked, Tina "Karate Girl" Green had been standing on a desk in the far corner, checking the high knickknack shelf. No worries there—Karate Girl was one of the best athletes in class. But now she teetered off-balance.

Tina was going to fall, hard, and no one was near enough to help.

Before I could even open my mouth to shout, a blur whizzed past me, heading for the corner desk. It vaulted a low table as Tina began to topple.

But this was a waste of time. No way could anyone reach her before she cracked her head on the nearest desk. Tina's eyes went wild and scared as she tumbled.

I winced, waiting for the impact.

And then, just before Tina hit—*schoomp!*—the strong

arms of Mr. Chu scooped her up. Her face was pure amazement.

I gaped. *Mr. Chu* had raced all the way across the classroom and saved her, in, like, two seconds? Seriously? The same Mr. Chu who claimed that jelly doughnuts were a major food group and that he hid from exercise because he was in the Fitness Protection Program?

What was going on here?

The whole class gathered around, drawn by the excitement.

"Way to go, Mr. Chu!" Big Pete pounded his thick hands together, and everyone joined the applause.

"Wow, you're so fast!" Amrita gushed.

"Uh, thanks, guys," said our teacher. He blushed, but under his embarrassment I thought I read confusion, like he wasn't quite sure how he'd done it.

He wasn't the only one.

Later, as our class filed out the door to go to lunch, Benny fell in beside me. "What's the deal with Mr. C?" he muttered, glancing around.

I checked behind us. Our teacher was still at the back of the line, out of earshot. "Beats me," I said. "All of a sudden he's Mr. Sniffy."

"And his hair grows like a time-lapse plant," said Benny.

"And he's faster than a speeding bullet. Do you think maybe . . . ?"

Benny nodded. "Of course. It's obvious."

"What is?"

"He's becoming a superhero."

My face scrunched up. "Seriously? Then what's with all the hair?"

"Well, maybe he's becoming a furry superhero, like Wolverine or Black Panther."

I frowned. "I think Black Panther wears tights. And Wolverine—"

"Doesn't matter." Benny waved away my doubts. "We've got to research this, pronto, and there's only one place for that."

"Yup."

"The comics store," we said together.

Chapter Two

Alarming News from Amazing Fred's

ITS ACTUAL NAME was Amazing Fred's Comix &
More, but everyone called it the comics store. The
green-and-black building stood just off Main Street,
sandwiched between a real estate office and one of those
shops that sell fruity-smelly soaps to moms.

As soon as the last school bell rang, Benny and I practically ran to the store. Yes, it would've been awesomely cool
if our teacher really *was* becoming a superhero. *Super-Chu—
he grades twenty tests with a single stroke! No PTA can withstand
his might!*

But I wasn't sure.

Mr. Chu had been acting so strange all day, it had me worried. I thought he might have a freaky brain tumor or some exotic disease. (Okay, I hadn't worked out how a disease could give you superfast reactions, but still.) Or if he was turning into something, it might be something a lot less . . . super. Like an alien pod person, for example.

We just *had* to know. And a comics store was a good place to start.

When Benny and I opened the door, the first two bars of Darth Vader's theme music played from a speaker deep inside the store, like always. Amazing Fred's was long, low, and rectangular, kinda like a shoe box. Murals along each wall mixed popular superheroes like Spider-Man and Batman with vampires, zombies, and a wide assortment of monsters.

Games, cards, collectibles, and magic books jammed every space not filled by rows of bins holding comics and graphic novels. I wouldn't say the comics store is our home away from home. But I will say that Benny and I have blown more allowance money there than in all the candy shops in town, combined.

As we entered, three high school students were thumbing through graphic novels in the back, snickering and talking together in low voices. The rich smell of expensive coffee drifted through the air. On the wall, the painted image of Predator caught my eye, and my stomach tightened.

What if Mr. Chu was becoming something like that?

"Howzit, boys? Help you with something?"

Back behind the glass cases where they keep all the really pricey stuff, I spotted the owner, Mrs. Tamasese. She'd bought the place from Amazing Fred a few years ago but liked the name so much she'd kept it.

"No, thanks," said Benny. "We're good."

"We are?" I said. "We don't even know where to start."

Benny cocked his head. "Sure we do. Follow me!" And he plunged into the bins of comics the way he plunges into most things—blindly and without a second thought.

Me, I like second, third, and sometimes even fourth thoughts. A guy can't be too careful.

Heading straight to the Incredible Hulk section, Benny pulled out the first volume of collected comics. He swatted it with the back of a hand. "Origin story."

"Yeah," I said. "So?"

Benny gave me his man-are-you-slow look. "It tells how radiation changed Bruce Banner into the Hulk. Duh. If we look up all superheroes created by radiation, we can see if Mr. Chu's symptoms match."

"You mean, like Spider-Man, Fantastic Four, and those guys?"

"Exactly."

I frowned, and my eyes strayed to the bookshelves where Mrs. Tamasese keeps the magic and supernatural books. "But how would someone in Monterrosa get zapped by radiation?"

Benny shrugged impatiently. "Drinking contaminated water, getting bit by a spider, eating a nuclear muffin—the usual."

"But what if there *was* no radiation?" I said. "What if Mr. Chu's sick?"

"Don't be morbid," Benny scoffed.

"Or what if he's not becoming a superhero?"

"How do you mean?" he asked.

I lowered my voice. "What if it's something worse?"

He spread his hands. "Then we check that out next. Jeez, Carlos, don't be a worrywart. Go grab *Spider-Man* Volume One. Chop-chop!"

When Benny gets into his bossy mood, sometimes it's easier to just play along. I wandered down the row, searching for the Spidey comics. Eyes on the bins, I was startled when something smacked my shoulder and spun me halfway around.

"Watch it, wetback." One of the high school kids towered over me. He was pale and pogo-stick skinny, with greasy hair and enough zits to make a relief map of the Rockies.

"Um, sorry," I mumbled.

What a punk. I burned to tell this too-tall dweeb that I'd been born right here in California, and that even my dad hadn't been born in Mexico. But I couldn't get the words out.

The puffy-eyed girl with him sneered. "Nerd alert!"

I wanted to point out that she and her friends were in the same store as me, so technically, they were nerds, too. But this didn't seem like the wisest move.

I cut my eyes toward Benny, but he was far down the row, leaning over a bin. No help there.

The high schoolers' chuckles grew nastier. "Aw, what's wrong, little taco nerd?" said Pogo Stick.

"You kids lost?"

Mrs. Tamasese's voice was low and calm, but the three jerks gave a guilty start and stepped back.

"Whaddaya mean 'lost'?" said Puffy-Eyed Girl.

The store owner wheeled up to them. "Earlier, I heard you say comics are for babies, and that you only read graphic novels." She pointed to the rear of the store. "Which are back there."

Cowed, the three kids skulked away without another word. You might not think a woman in a wheelchair could be intimidating, but you would be wrong.

Mrs. Tamasese is the most famous person I've ever met. My dad says that years ago, she used to wrestle for WOW (Women of Wrestling, if you've never watched it) as the Samoan Slammer. But then she got hurt or something and she's been rocking it from a purple wheelchair ever since.

She still looks like a superhero from the waist up.

"Doing some research?" she asked me.

"Uh, yeah," I said. "Thanks for—"

Mrs. Tamasese brushed aside my thanks as if scaring off snotty teens was part of her job. (And maybe it was.) "What are you investigating?" she asked.

I liked that she said *investigating*, like I was Sherlock Holmes or something. But suddenly I felt a little silly.

"Our teacher . . . umm . . ."

From down the row, Benny cut in, waving a comic book. "Superspeed, check," he called. "Nothing about supersmell, though."

Patient and steady, Mrs. Tamasese kept her gaze on me.

"Our, um, teacher started acting funny today," I said. "And we were, uh, worried."

Her eyes slipped off my face, focusing on something behind me.

"Never mind," I said. "It was a dumb—"

"Be right back," said Mrs. Tamasese. She popped a wheelie and whipped along the aisle.

Turning, I saw the three high schoolers strolling toward the door. Pogo Stick's jacket was zipped up, and one elbow seemed glued to his ribs. His innocent expression wouldn't have fooled a kindergartner.

I picked up Volume One of *The Amazing Spider-Man* and started leafing through it for clues. At least Mr. Chu wasn't shooting gunk out of his wrists. Yet.

But the real-life drama drew my attention.

"Forgetting something?" Mrs. Tamasese rolled up beside Pogo Stick. She thumped the back of her hand against his side, and it made a *thonk* I could hear across the store.

Busted.

The kid tensed up and gathered himself to flee. Mrs. Tamasese grabbed his wrist. "Book, please," she said.

With a sheepish look, Pogo Stick slipped the graphic novel from under his jacket and handed it over. I recognized the pink cover from across the room.

"Babymouse?" I said before I could stop myself. "My little sister reads . . ."

Pogo Stick had a good glare. I shut my mouth with a

snap. *Stupid, stupid Carlos. This is why we think twice before speaking.*

Mrs. Tamasese cleared her throat. Pogo Stick and his friends slunk out the door. If they'd had tails, they would've been tucked between their legs.

The store owner wheeled her way back to me. "So, your teacher," she said. "What kind of funny behavior?"

I put down the Spider-Man and filled her in. She listened intently, her brown eyes serious. I liked that she was the kind of grown-up who actually knew how to connect with kids.

"Maybe he's sick," said Mrs. Tamasese at last.

I tilted my head. "I thought so, too, but what kind of sickness makes you superstrong and fast?"

She made a face. "Good point. And you say he reacted to the smell of your dog?"

"Yeah. Almost like he hated it." A thought struck me. "Hey, is there some superhero who turns into a cat?"

The store owner shook her head. "No actual cats. Catwoman doesn't count."

Just then, Benny turned up at my side. "I've checked Hulk and Fantastic Four," he said. "Nobody's growing hair after getting blasted with gamma rays."

"That's because your teacher isn't turning into a superhero," said Mrs. Tamasese.

"Oh, no?" said Benny. He sounded defensive. "Then what's wrong with him?"

"Not sure yet," she said, crooking a finger at us. "Come on."

Mrs. Tamasese's shoulder muscles bunched as she expertly spun her wheelchair toward the paranormal section of the store. *Ay*, you wouldn't want to get on her bad side, I thought. One punch, and—*pow!*—out like a light.

"I used to live in New Orleans, among other places," said Mrs. Tamasese, scanning the book spines. "And unless I'm reading it wrong, your teacher might be turning into some supernatural creature."

I felt my eyebrows scale my forehead like a pair of mountain-climbing caterpillars. Did the store owner really believe in that kind of stuff?

"What, like Bigfoot?" asked Benny.

"Bigfoot's not supernatural," I said.

"Well, he's not *real*," said Benny.

I blew out a sigh. We'd always disagreed about cryptids like Bigfoot. Benny thinks they're fake, like unicorns or fairies; I think no one's been able to capture them on film yet.

Mrs. Tamasese reached for a really old-looking book. "No, I'm talking about creatures like what New Orleans folk call the *loup-garou*."

"The loogey-roo?" Benny's nose wrinkled.

"What's that?" I asked. "Some kind of snot-monster?"

She flipped through the pages. "Not quite. There should a be a picture . . . ah, here we go."

Mrs. Tamasese held up the book so we could see.

"Nah," said Benny.

"Seriously?" I asked.

The store owner looked as grim as the first school day after winter vacation. "Yes, gentlemen. There's a chance that your teacher is becoming what's commonly called a werewolf."

"A *werewolf*?" said Benny.

I sagged against the bookshelf. "I *really* would've preferred a superhero."

Chapter Three

Odd Plan Out

"**B**UT IT'S ONLY a chance, right?" I said. "Mr. Chu isn't *for sure* turning into a wolfman, is he?"

I really didn't want to lose my favorite teacher ever. To say nothing of the fact that if he bit me, I'd become a werewolf, too—and I wasn't sure how my parents would take that.

"Too early to say," said Mrs. Tamasese. She flipped through a few more pages, and then reshelved the book with a sigh. "There are so many different kinds of shapeshifters—panthers, wolves, jackals, bears, sharks. . . ."

"Were-sharks?" said Benny, his eyes widening. "Really? That's a thing now?" Like me, he'd been a bit spooked by that shark movie.

Suddenly the Darth Vader theme played, and I'm not ashamed to say I jumped a little.

"I don't have the right books here," said Mrs. Tamasese,

glancing over at her newest customer, a helmet-haired man in a navy-blue suit. "Gotta check my personal collection tonight. Can you come around tomorrow, after school?"

"Yeah, but—" I began.

"What do we do about Mr. Chu in the meantime?" Benny asked.

Mrs. Tamasese was already wheeling herself toward the customer, who stood with his hands folded together, smiling expectantly. "Watch him carefully," she tossed over her shoulder, "but don't get too close until we know what's what."

"Don't get too close to our teacher?" I said.

"Right," said Benny. "That shouldn't be a problem."

"Sure," I said. "We only spend six hours a day with him. No problem I can see."

We hung around awhile longer, but Mrs. Tamasese had her hands full—first with Mr. Helmet Hair, who'd placed a huge order of magic supplies, even though he didn't look much like a magician. Then came a steady stream of other customers who needed her help.

After browsing through the supernatural section and not finding much about shapeshifters, Benny and I headed home. As we passed through downtown Monterrosa and peeled off into our neighborhood, we discussed our options.

"We can't wait for Mrs. T to help us," said Benny.

"Why not?" I was all in favor of getting some assistance on this one. The more, the better.

Benny grimaced. "You kidding? After how weird Mr. Chu was today? We'll be lucky if he doesn't go full-frontal wolf—"

"Or bear," I said.

"—or panther, or wildebeest, or whatever," he said, "by lunch tomorrow. There's no time. We've gotta be proactive."

Benny and I crossed the street to avoid the house with the Rottweiler that often got loose.

"'Proactive'?" I said.

He shrugged. "It's what my dad says when he's on a case—'Can't be reactive, gotta be proactive.'"

Benny's dad, Albert Brackman, was the head detective for the Monterrosa police. He was a smart, tough guy, and full of wise sayings like that.

"Okay," I said. "But since we don't know whether Mr. Chu is turning into a coyote, a panda, or Miss Muffet's spider, what kind of proactivity do you suggest?"

Benny was silent for a few strides, a rare thing for him. We cut through the Little League diamonds, empty except for two girls playing catch.

"Research," he said at last. "Mrs. Tamasese said he's probably becoming a shapeshifter, right?"

"Right."

"So we Google 'cures for shapeshifters' or something

like that. Maybe the different cures have something in common."

I saw what he was driving at. "And if we find some cure that's the same for werewolves, were-panthers, and were-whatevers, we try it on Mr. Chu."

"Bingo," said Benny. "Houston, we have a plan."

"Don't do the Houston thing," I said.

"What?" said Benny. Ever since he saw that space movie, it'd been "Houston this" and "Houston that." Don't get me wrong—Benny's great, but he can really overdo a catchphrase.

We headed for my place, since, thanks to my dad's work, we have the faster computers. Banging through the front door, I called out, "Hey, Abuelita! We're home."

The honk of her saxophone cut off, midphrase. My grandma's voice reached us from the living room, "*Hola, mijo*. Don't slam the—"

Wham! The door blew shut behind us.

"Sorry!" Benny and I chorused.

Woof-woof-woof! With a clatter of toenails on wood floor, my dog, Zeppo, came running up to cover us with slobber. His ears flopped, and his wavy blond-brown fur seemed to be on auto-shed mode. After accepting his doggie kisses, I thumped his flanks and scratched him behind his ears, the way he likes it.

My grandma appeared in the living room doorway. "You boys . . ."

"I'll remember next time," I said. "Promise."

The look on her face said she believed me about as much as she had the last 287 times I'd said that. Still, she came up and kissed my cheek.

"I'm practicing for our next gig," she said. "You boys hungry? Want something?" My *abuela* played sax in a ska band. Her solos were even hotter than her salsa.

"We've got a lot of research—uh, homework to do," I said.

"But I wouldn't say no to some of your empanadas." Benny gave my grandma his angelic smile. She fell for it, as always.

"Ay, Benito," she said, patting his cheek. "You're too skinny. Pumpkin empanadas, coming right up."

It always seemed to make Abuelita happy to cook for us. And who were we to mess with her happiness?

I led Benny to our family room. My dad's hand-me-down computer, a slick iMac, was perched on a desk, surrounded by snowdrifts of papers and magazines. The room smelled of roast chicken and wet dog. (Not surprising, since that was where Zeppo liked to hang out and chew stuff. Including chicken.)

After a good hour of research and a full plate of empanadas, we discovered three very important things:

1. Most shapeshifting cures date back to the Middle Ages, when sticking nails into someone's hands or

hitting them on the head with a knife was considered a good thing;

2. The Internet is full of distractions (did you know there's a guy called Cat Man, who's actually had surgery and gotten his face tattooed to look like a tiger?); and

3. My grandma's empanadas are irresistible.

But we also found one idea that Benny was eager to try on Mr. Chu.

"Looks like surgery might work," he said.

I gave him my you've-got-to-be-kidding face. "Surgery?"

"What?" he said.

"You seriously think Mr. Chu will let us operate on him?"

"Why not?"

"I'm your best friend, and I'm not sure I'd trust you to take out a splinter with tweezers," I said. "So he's supposed to just let us hack away at him, in front of the whole class?"

Benny frowned. "Okay, I didn't think that through. But maybe we could talk him into letting a doctor do it?"

"Dream on."

"Okay, scratch surgery."

I scrolled down the browser window and clicked on a link. "Ooh, how about we exorcise him?"

Benny's nose scrunched up. "You mean, take him for a run?"

"Not exercise, ex*or*cise. You know, when they drive the evil spirits out?"

"Like in that movie *The Exorcist*?" he asked. "With the priests and the cross and the girl's head spinning around?"

"Not exactly." I read further. "Looks like there are all kinds of exorcism to cast out demons and heal shapeshifters."

"Let's do it, then," said Benny.

"The only problem is, how do we pull it off?"

"What do you mean?" he asked.

I rolled my eyes. "We can't just walk up to him and say, 'Hold still, we're gonna exorcise you.'"

Benny's forehead crinkled. "Hmm . . ."

We stared at each other, stumped. Then his face lit up. "Hey, we could slip it into our social studies project!"

"I dunno . . ." I said. Our project, due tomorrow, was supposed to be about the origin of fireworks. "Exorcism and fireworks?"

"Don't worry," said Benny. "I'll handle everything."

I had my doubts. But desperate times call for desperate measures. "Okay," I said. "Let's round up some exorcism things from a few different cultures. That way it'll look more like a real report."

Benny rubbed his hands together. "Excellent! I'm almost sure I can borrow a chicken or two from our neighbors."

"A chicken?"

"Yeah, for sacrificing and stuff," he said.

"No chickens," I said. "No sacrifices."

"Right. We'll use a goat."

"No goats."

We spent another hour gathering and organizing the materials we'd need. When we'd finished, it was almost dinnertime. Before Benny went home, I looked over everything we'd collected and all the research we'd done.

"You know," I said, "if we put this much effort into our homework, we'd probably be getting straight As."

"And if the water fountains ran with chocolate milk," said Benny, "I'd drink two gallons a day. Get real, Carlos. Homework is *never* this much fun."

Dinner that night was a quiet one, just me and Abuelita at first. Dad had to work late, and Mom and my little sister, Veronica, were still down in L.A. for her audition. Oh, yeah, my six-year-old sister wanted to be an actress. And my stagestruck mom wanted to make sure she got what she wanted—even if it meant driving Veronica five hours to a silly tryout.

Honestly, if you have a choice, don't be the oldest kid. The parents use up all their strictness on the firstborn, and by the time the second one comes around, they let them do anything.

The younger ones always have it easier.

I must have been wearing a worried look, because my grandma asked, "Anything wrong, *mijo?*"

"Not really." Not that I could talk about anyway. I tilted my head. "Do you believe in the supernatural?"

She snorted a laugh. "You mean vampires and zombies and ghosts?"

"And, uh, stuff like that."

"Ay, Carlito." Abuelita ruffled my hair. "My mother's *mole*, a glorious sunset, a blazing sax solo—that's supernatural. But ghosts?" She chuckled again. "*¡Qué imaginación!*"

I wished it *were* just my imagination. But the other kids had seen Mr. Chu's crazy antics, too.

Abuelita and I were halfway finished eating by the time Dad showed up, looking like one of Zeppo's old chew toys. He joined us at the table and picked at his dinner, distracted. But he still made sure to ask me the usual parent questions.

"What did you study today, Carlos?" Dad asked, toying with his enchilada. His hair was messy and his eyes looked tired.

"Oh, the usual stuff," I said. Exorcisms, *loup-garous*, and werewolf cures. "Nothing special."

"And what are you up to tomorrow?"

I wiped my mouth. "Um, Benny and I are going to present our social studies project." And try to cure our teacher from becoming a monster.

"Oh," said my dad, his eyes on some work papers and his mind a million miles away. "Good luck with that."

"Thanks, Dad," I said. "We sure could use it."

Chapter Four

Countdown to an Exorcism

THE NEXT MORNING, we had so much stuff to carry, Benny's mom volunteered to drive us to school. She dropped us by the flagpole, like all the other moms and dads, and blew Benny a kiss, which he ducked. It was an old routine with them.

"Have a successful day, boys!" she called to us. Mrs. Brackman is one of those up-with-people people, always saying things like, "It's Monday—don't forget to be awesome," "Be a warrior, not a worrier," or "My blood type is be positive."

It's nice, I guess. But a little goes a long way.

Benny and I hauled our gear—including his covered pet carrier, which was making suspicious noises—into the flow of kids heading for class. Tina Green fell in beside us.

"Hey, Brackman, Rivera," she said.

"Hey, Karate Girl," I said.

Tina had arrow-straight cornrows and braids with beads on them that clicked as she moved her head—*tik-tik-tik*. She'd also been taking karate lessons since she was three or something, so nobody *ever* teased her about her hair. Eyeballing our massive collection of bags and bundles, she asked, "You moving in?"

"Yup," said Benny. "Just can't get enough of school."

I shook my head. "Social studies project."

Tina patted her book bag. "Mine's in here. You guys might want to consider doing something simpler next time."

"Yeah." I traded looks with Benny. "If we could, we would."

Glancing to both sides, Tina lowered her voice. "Hey, what's with Mr. Chu? He was acting so weird yesterday."

"Really?" said Benny. "Hadn't noticed."

"Uh-huh." Tina arched an eyebrow. "'Cause most normal teachers growl and dash across the room in a flash. Riiight."

"Okay," I said, "he *was* a little weird. Maybe it was only a bad mood." I didn't know why, but I wasn't eager to discuss our shapeshifting theory with her.

"Uh-huh," Tina said again, like she didn't believe a word. "I'm sure that's all. Well, if you guys decide to let me in on it, just send a text."

And she lengthened her stride, pulling away from our weak protests and into the classroom.

"You think she knows?" Benny asked.

"She'd be a lot more worried if she did," I said.

I noticed that Benny hadn't volunteered our plans either. I wondered if he, like me, had a secret wish to be the hero, to save the day.

Room Thirteen was about half full. Kids were catching up with friends, doing last-minute homework, and getting ready for another school day. Mr. Chu wasn't around. But his coat hung on his chair, and his sustainable bamboo briefcase (which he'd told us all about during our ecology unit) sat on his desk.

Benny scanned the room. "Perfect timing!" He dumped his bags by his desk and rummaged through one of them. "I brought a little insurance, in case our you-know-what doesn't work."

"Insurance is good," I said.

Then Benny fished out a spray can with a whispered, "Ta-da!"

"No way," I whispered back. "You didn't."

With a broad smile and a waggle of his eyebrows, Benny hurried up to the teacher's desk with the canister. I followed on his heels.

"Benny, you can't—"

"Stand a little more over that way, to cover me," said Benny. He crouched, shook the can, and began spraying

Mr. Chu's jacket with Doggie-Off—the stuff you use to keep your dog from chewing on furniture and stuff.

Automatically, I moved to conceal him. "Seriously, Doggie-Off? We don't even know what he's turning into."

He lifted a shoulder. "So? If it's something doglike, or even something that hates dogs, it might work. A good dose might scare the whatever-it-is out of him."

"Or make him lose his breakfast," I said. The formula kind of stank.

After soaking the jacket, Benny went on to spritz the desktop. I checked out the room. A few kids were staring at us curiously.

"Enough," I muttered. "We've got an audience."

Benny pretended to wipe off Mr. Chu's desk. "And there we go," he said in a fake-cheery voice. "Spick-and-span."

"Teacher's pet," sneered Tyler Spork, who had just come in.

I didn't have a comeback, but Benny said, "Cleanliness is next to godliness, and godliness is next to good grades. Jealous much, Tyler?"

Tyler scowled, and we headed back to our desks. Just then, the bell rang. On the heels of the last few students, Mr. Chu burst through the door, a bundle of energy.

"Gooood morning, Monterrosa!" he boomed.

The class started to respond in the usual singsong way, but most of us faltered halfway through our "Good morning, Mr. Chu."

Why? His hair.

Yep. Bald-headed Mr. Chu now sported a crop of spiky black hair a good three inches long. He looked like a hedgehog that had stuck its paw in a light socket, and he was grinning like a lottery winner.

"It's another awesome day," he said, "and I can't wait to learn something new!" Then our teacher ripped out a long, high giggle. "Let's get edumacated!"

I turned to Benny. He looked just as concerned as I felt, and the rest of the class wore various shades of confusion on their faces.

Oblivious, Mr. Chu dived right into his first lesson, playing Base Ten Bingo with us like nothing was the matter. Benny and I kept an eye on his Doggie-Offed coat and desktop, but our teacher didn't even approach them. Instead, he roamed the aisles like a daytime-TV host, occasionally calling out "Bingo!" and giggling.

At the end of the lesson, Mr. Chu finally sat down. His nose crinkled, and he brought it right down to the desktop, sniffing deeply.

"Whew!" He fanned the air in front of his face. "I have to have a talk with the janitor."

"Or Benny," said Tyler.

"Or Benny," our teacher agreed. "'Cause someone unleashed a whole new kind of clean here." He cackled again, like he'd just said the funniest joke in the world, then plunged into a discussion of our class read, *Charlie and the Chocolate Factory*.

Clearly, the Doggie-Off wasn't working.

But on the other hand, Mr. Chu didn't seem particularly wolfy, aside from the extra hair. He was pretty cheerful. In fact, with all the wild laughter, he seemed a lot like a certain comic-book character. I scrawled a quick note:

Any chance he could be turning into The Joker?

And I folded it up and passed it to AJ, who handed it across to Benny. When Benny read it, he glanced at me and shook his head.

"Benny, you don't agree?" said Mr. Chu coldly.

"Uh, what now?" said Benny.

"With Cheyenne's point that our author condemns greed in this story. Are you some kind of illiterate moron? Did you even read the book?" As though his mean switch had just been flipped, our teacher grew flinty-eyed, and his lips peeled back from his teeth in a snarl.

Benny looked like he'd been slapped. I gaped. Had our kindly Mr. Chu just slammed my friend?

"Well?" our teacher demanded. "Are you a mute, too?"

Benny held up his hands in a surrendering gesture. "Um, no. I agree one hundred percent," he said, voice wavering.

"Then why shake your head?" our teacher barked.

"Um, a fly was bothering me?" said Benny.

"Flies?" Mr. Chu's snarl disappeared, replaced by keen interest. He sniffed the air eagerly. "Is there something dead or rotten around here?"

"Yeah," said Tyler. "Benny's lunch."

The class laughed. But it was a nervous laughter. Most of us were rattled by Mr. Chu's bizarre mood swing from Dr. Giggle to Mr. Snide. Our teacher snuffled awhile longer, and then, disappointed, got back to the discussion.

Benny sneaked a glance at me. Worry carved new lines in his face.

I gnawed my lip. Whatever Mr. Chu was turning into, he was no longer the friendly, funny Teacher of the Year we'd come to know and love. Something *was* rotten, and it wasn't Benny's lunch (although to be honest, he ate stuff that I wouldn't touch).

Benny was right. We had to do something.

Right after recess, Mr. Chu asked, "Who would like to go first with their social studies project?"

I looked over at Benny. We exchanged a tense nod.

I raised my hand.

Showtime.

Chapter Five

Chickening Out

YOU CAN'T RUSH an exorcism. It took a couple of minutes for us to haul everything to the front of the room and set it up. Throughout, Mr. Chu seemed particularly interested in the draped pet carrier. His sniffer was working overtime.

Finally, we were ready.

I cleared my throat. Public speaking didn't seem quite as scary now that there were bigger things at stake. (Plus I had a partner who loved to talk.)

"Our, uh, report was supposed to be about fireworks," I began, holding up a sparkler. "Fun fact: they were first used at celebrations to bring good luck and chase off evil spirits." I shot a look at Benny.

He took my handoff. "But as we researched, we found the whole getting-rid-of-evil-spirits thing totally fascinating."

"Totally," I said.

"More fascinating than fireworks. So now our report is about . . . exorcism around the world!" Benny held out his hands in a ta-da! gesture.

Big Pete frowned. "Exercising?"

"Exorcism," Benny and I said together. I checked on Mr. Chu.

His expression landed somewhere between amused and confused. "Hmm. Not quite the same as—*hee-hee*—fireworks." He was back to being Dr. Giggle again.

"True," I said. "But we put a lot of work into it."

"Then—*hee-hee-hee*—go ahead," said Mr. Chu. His fingers scratched furiously at his cheek like a dog with fleas.

With a wary glance at our teacher, Benny hefted one of his dad's sturdy walking sticks. "In Buddhist cultures, they used three things to cast out demons. . . ."

"First, incense," I said.

I lit a stick that we'd borrowed from Benny's mom and paraded it around like a torch. A sweet, woody smell began to fill the room. When I waved the incense under Mr. Chu's nose to give him a good dose, he sneezed.

"Next, religious verses," said Benny. "Um, we can't read Japanese, so I made up one of my own:

> *Demon, demon, go away*
> *Don't come back another day*
> *Beat it, scram, and let him be*
> *Cheese it, freeze it, one-two-three!*

As he said the final lines, I twirled the incense around Mr. Chu's head and shoulders and stood back. We watched him expectantly.

A funny look crept over his face.

Then, in a manic burst, our teacher giggled and sneezed simultaneously, which sounded something like, *"Aahhh-hee-hee-hee-CHOO-heh!"*

Not quite what we were hoping for.

Some of our classmates laughed. Others shook their heads, or looked down as though embarrassed for us.

"The final part of the Buddhist cure," I said, "is making a loud noise with a big stick."

At this, Benny hoisted the walking stick over his head and thwacked it down on Mr. Chu's desk. Once, twice! With the third *thwack*, our teacher's coffee cup jumped, and he had to grab it to prevent a spill.

"Enough sticks!" growled Mr. Chu. His lips peeled back in a wicked snarl, and his face went tomato red. "I hate sticks!"

Eyes wide, Benny put away the cane.

Mr. Chu definitely wasn't his normal self yet, so I motioned at Benny to continue.

"Christians also have a long tradition of exorcising witches, devils, werewolves, and all that kind of stuff," he said.

"Cool," said Tyler. Then, recognizing he'd actually expressed interest in something, he scowled. "I mean, it would be, if it wasn't totally lame."

Benny and I dug into one of our bags. "Priests use a combination of prayers, symbols, and holy water to drive out demons," I said.

In a rush, we produced a wooden cross I'd borrowed from my grandma, a Bible, and a Super Soaker squirt gun. I brandished the Bible and cross at Mr. Chu, the way vampire hunters do in the movies.

Benny squirted the gun, first at our classmates, then over at Mr. Chu. Kids squealed. Our teacher recoiled, and Benny and I recited the only prayer we knew by heart:

> *Now I lay me down to sleep,*
> *I pray the Lord my soul to keep;*
> *If I should die before I wake,*
> *I pray the Lord my soul to take!*

This time, Mr. Chu's reaction was instantaneous. "Enough squirting!" he barked, looking fiercer than ever.

"Sorry," I said. "We got carried away." Although I watched him like a hawk, Mr. Chu didn't start steaming where the holy water had hit him. He wasn't speaking in some demonic gobbledygook language or rotating his head. In fact, he looked exactly like a wet, annoyed teacher.

Guess you can't believe everything you see in the movies.

"Okay, then," said Benny. "Our last exorcism cure comes from the Caribbean."

I turned to look at him. "It does?"

"Does it involve pirates?" asked Tina, who was nuts about pirate movies.

"Nope, voodoo," said Benny.

The class went "Ooh!" Now, I knew from my dad's Cuban friend Lorenzo that Vodoun was an actual religion and not some mumbo jumbo of voodoo dolls and zombies. But most people have no clue.

"It's actually called Vod—" I began.

"In the voodoo culture, they use graveyard dirt to make their exorcism strong," said Benny, reaching into the sack and flinging handfuls of dirt on the floor around Mr. Chu's desk.

"They don't actually—" I said.

"Hey, now," said our teacher, sounding like himself for a moment. "You're cleaning that up."

But Benny didn't pause for a second. He was on a roll.

"The voodoo priests shake a sacred gourd." Here he waved a rattle that looked suspiciously like the one his parents had brought back from their vacation in Acapulco.

"And then comes"—Benny whisked the cover off the pet carrier and opened its door—"the sacrifice!"

Two chickens burst through the opening, squawking their heads off.

"Whoa!" I said. "You're not really gonna—"

Spouting a wild, fake witch-doctor chant, Benny produced

a pair of scissors and lunged for the nearest chicken. Being a chicken, it *bwaak*ed in alarm, beat its wings, and fluttered up onto Mr. Chu's desk. The other bird flew straight out, landing in Zizi's lap.

She gave a surprised shriek, and the class erupted. Some kids scrambled away from the chicken, some tried to catch it. Chasing after the bird flapping about on Mr. Chu's desk, Benny yelled, "Carlos! Help me!"

"You're beyond help," I said. But I followed him anyway.

Benny grabbed and missed. The bird fluttered up and landed on the far edge of the desk. There it sat, clucking in an offended way. Benny stalked around the desk after it.

Mr. Chu's eyes were as round as volleyballs. He gazed at the chicken the way Zeppo stares at squirrels, and his whole body vibrated with tension. Both he and Benny were totally focused on that bird. Then . . .

Schoomp!

Just as both of them started to make their move, a figure shot across the desk, scooping up the chicken and landing in a crouch on the other side.

Karate Girl.

Benny and Mr. Chu knocked heads in the empty space where the chicken had been. The scissors fell on the floor. Benny looked dazed.

Our teacher recovered first. Wheeling on Tina with a crazed gleam in his eyes, he grabbed greedily for the bird.

You don't take several years' worth of karate classes

without learning some serious moves. Tina ducked and twisted, keeping the chicken out of reach.

"Gimme!" our teacher demanded.

"No." Tina sent me a silent appeal.

"Um, Mr. Chu," I said, "Tina's got it under control."

"My chicken!" he roared. "*My* chicken! Ah-*hee-hee-hee*!" In a lightning-fast lunge, he managed to snatch a fistful of feathers.

Buh-kwaaak! went the bird. Karate Girl danced sideways, putting the desk between her and our chicken-crazy teacher.

"Calm down, Mr. Chu," she said.

"I . . . am . . . calm!" he cried. Without warning, he dived across his desk, both hands outstretched. This time, our teacher caught Tina by the wrists. She struggled.

"Ow!" cried Karate Girl. "You're hurting me!"

Mr. Chu didn't even hear her. He sprawled halfway across his desk, trying to tug Tina closer and snapping his jaws at the freaked-out bird in her grasp. I wrapped my arms around Tina's waist and planted my feet to hold her back, but he was impossibly strong.

The expression on Mr. Chu's face was purely bestial, all savage appetite.

He dragged us closer . . . closer . . .

Fweeeet! A whistle blast cut through the uproar.

Everyone stopped what they were doing and turned to

look at the source of the sound. Standing in the doorway, her whistle still in hand, was a lanky brown woman in a powder-blue pantsuit and cowboy boots. Our principal, Mrs. Johnson.

"Now, what in the Sam Hill is going on here?" she said.

Chapter Six

Principal Charming

THERE ARE TWO theories on how to handle principals. Neither one works. After a brief introductory scolding from Mrs. Johnson, we braced ourselves for the inevitable.

Even with help, it took about ten minutes to collect our supplies and cram the chickens back into their carrier. After that, we went on one of the scariest trips at school: straight up to the principal's office. (I wish I could tell you that Benny and I had never been there before, but my *abuela* says it's not good to lie.)

We sat on the hard plastic chairs by the attendance desk. As usual, the office smelled of home-baked brownies, Magic Markers, and fear.

"That could've gone a little better," said Benny.

"You think?" I said.

"Maybe if we'd gotten to sacrifice the chickens—"

I broke in. "We'd be in even more trouble than we're in now." I glanced at the school secretary, Mrs. Garcia. She was typing away on her computer, pretending to ignore us, but I knew she could hear every word we said. Secretaries and teachers have ears like bats.

The last thing we needed was to have wild talk of were-creatures spread through the school. But *Benny* and *cautious* are two words that don't go together.

"And after all that exorcising, he's still a—" Benny began.

"Very patient teacher." I cut my eyes toward Mrs. Garcia, but Benny was distracted and didn't catch it.

He rubbed his palms together. "Guess we'll have to try another cure for—"

"Your *dog's* case of *heartworm*," I said, glaring. At Benny's puzzled look, I tilted my head toward the secretary, who had stopped typing and was doing her best not to gawk at us.

At last, Benny got it.

"Ah, yes!" he exclaimed. "Bummer that the heartburn cure didn't work."

"Heart*worm*," I muttered.

"So we should go visit the, uh, *pet store* after school."

Benny's eyebrows waggled like he was sending me a Morse-code message. He may have been my best friend, but subtle he wasn't.

I rolled my eyes.

Just then, Mrs. Johnson's door opened and Mr. Chu stepped out, in midsentence. ". . . all just a—*hee-hee-hee*—misunderstanding," he was saying.

"I'm sure it was," the principal drawled. She rested a hand on her office doorframe and snuck a quick glance at Mr. Chu's formerly bald scalp. "But if you need a little time out because of stress or . . ."

Our teacher shook off her concern. "Not me. Never felt better, ha ha!" And with a cheery wave to Mrs. Johnson and an unreadable glance at Benny and me, he swept out the side door.

The principal's gaze landed on us. My stomach dropped into my socks.

"Boys," she said, "come in."

I followed Benny into the office and sat in one of the culprit chairs designed for guilty visitors. You could tell they were culprit chairs because they were hard enough to make you confess to almost anything. But somehow, I didn't think confessing the real reason for our exorcism would be a good idea.

Not yet. Not till we knew more.

Mrs. Johnson shut her door and strode to the other side

of her desk. She stood there, watching us, not speaking. A slim woman with short, curly hair, Mrs. Johnson must have studied the Principal Stare back where she came from in Texas, because she had it down pat.

It felt like fire ants wearing golf cleats were crawling over my skin.

After what seemed like an hour, Mrs. Johnson said, "So?"

"We didn't do it! We're innocent!" Benny burst out. "It wasn't our fault."

I bit my lip. He'd forgotten the first rule of dealing with principals: never volunteer information.

One eyebrow climbed her forehead. "You didn't turn those chickens loose?"

"Well," I said, "technically, we did."

"But we didn't mean to," said Benny. "It just got out of hand."

"And the"—Mrs. Johnson consulted a notepad on her desk—"dirt, the squirt guns, and the whacking things with sticks?"

I shrugged apologetically.

"All an accident?" said Benny. "We were superexcited about our project. Things got a little messy."

The principal's lips tightened into a straight line.

"We were only trying to give our social studies report," I said. "Honest."

"Other students make their reports without disrupting the entire classroom," Mrs. Johnson said. "You're fourth graders now. I had hoped for better judgment from you."

I winced. "We're really, really sorry."

"Really, really," added Benny.

The principal's stare went from one of us to the other. "I could forgive nearly everything but the doggone chickens. Tell me true: Whose idea were they?" She turned the full force of the Principal Stare on me.

My breath stopped. It was all Benny's idea, of course, but you never rat out your buddies. That was the second rule of dealing with principals.

The silence stretched.

"Um," said Benny, shifting in his seat.

"We both came up with it," I blurted. Benny shot me a grateful glance. "But we never thought they'd escape."

"Carlos." Mrs. Johnson frowned. "You're a good student. I expected more of you."

Did that mean she expected less of Benny?

"Sorry." My ears burned and I couldn't look her in the eye. "It won't happen again."

"You're darn tootin'," she said. Mrs. Johnson gazed at us awhile longer. It looked like she was making up her mind about whether to throw us in the dungeon, stretch us on the rack, or tie us to an anthill.

Finally, she said, "You'll both serve detention today, and

I don't want you leaving one speck of your mess for the janitor. Not one chicken feather, not one dirt clod. Clear?"

"Yes, ma'am," we chorused.

"Go on, now." She made a shooing motion, and we stood up to leave.

Then a thought struck me. Maybe she deserved to know something about our teacher's problem, if not the whole truth. "Um, Mrs. Johnson?" I said.

"Yes, Carlos?"

"Have you . . ." How to say this without sounding like a wacko? "Have you noticed anything different about Mr. Chu recently?"

"Different?" Her other eyebrow arched up her forehead. I wished I could do that.

"You know, strange?" I said. "Weird?"

Mrs. Johnson angled her head. "You're talking about a teacher who dresses up as Dr. Frankenstein, Genghis Khan, and a giant cucumber? *Strange* isn't the word. He's nuttier than a boxful of woodpeckers."

"No, but see—" Benny began.

"And he's one of my best teachers," said the principal. "Don't try to blame Mr. Chu. He may have overreacted in the heat of the moment, but this is all your doing."

"But—" Benny tried again.

"Don't let the door hit you on the way out," said Mrs. Johnson, sitting down at her desk and turning her attention to some reports. She used folksy Texas sayings like that sometimes, but what she really meant in this case was *beat it*.

So we beat it.

Mr. Chu grew more demented as the day went on. He kept laughing like a maniac at things that weren't funny. That wasn't so bad, but he completely lost his sense of humor at the same time. He bullied Zizi until he drove her to tears, and he mocked Big Pete's learning disability in front of the whole class. That was totally uncool.

Luckily, he didn't attack any other students or chickens, but I guessed it was only a matter of time. Our teacher was a ticking time bomb of weirdness. I couldn't wait to go hear if Mrs. Tamasese had figured out what Mr. Chu was turning into.

But school being school, I had to.

Not long before the end of the day, the upper grades got called into an assembly. Usually, assemblies were boring with a capital *B*—a chance for teachers to gossip and kids to snooze while some grown-up with a microphone went blah, blah, blah. But not today.

Standing beside Mrs. Johnson as she gave her usual, keep-your-lips-zipped introduction was a familiar-looking man. He had slick, perfect black hair, like he'd greased it and then combed it back with a steel-toothed comb and a T square. He was as tanned as a tennis player in July. And he wore a sharp-looking navy-blue suit.

"It's the same guy," I told Benny.

"Who?" he asked.

"Mr. Helmet Hair. We saw him at the comics store."

"Who?"

I pointed at the front of the multipurpose room. "That guy. He came in just before we left, asking about magic supplies."

Benny shook his head. "I can't believe it."

"What, that I have such a good memory?" I asked.

"No, that you name people like that. What do you call our principal, Mrs. Kangaroo Boots?" He nodded at Mrs. Johnson's fancy cowboy footwear.

Then our principal said, "Please give a warm Monterrosa Elementary welcome to Mr. Sharkawy of the Monterrosa Art Museum." Everyone clapped, in that halfhearted way you do when you have no clue who the person is and you're just being polite.

The helmet-haired man took a long moment to survey us. He had dark, penetrating eyes, an eagle's beak of a nose, and a mysterious half smile.

"Magic," he said, "is all around us."

"So are germs," muttered Benny. I stifled a chuckle.

"Monsters . . . are all around us," Mr. Sharkawy continued, raking the audience with his eyes. Benny and I both perked up at that.

"Is he talking about . . . ?" I whispered.

Mr. Sharkawy clapped and, with a flash of sparks, a

great cloud of purple smoke blossomed. When it cleared, a tall glass display case stood on the formerly bare stage beside him.

An "oooh" arose from the crowd.

"Nice trick," Benny said sarcastically. But I could tell he was impressed.

The museum guy allowed himself a tiny smile, then continued. "Sub-Saharan African societies, like the Yoruba, Bakongo, and Dan, have long recognized the existence of the supernatural. Just because our culture pooh-poohs it doesn't mean it's not real. The supernatural is as real as a wolf howl, as real as this display case. And it's still here with us today."

Nervous laughter greeted his remark.

Sliding open the glass front of the case, Mr. Sharkawy removed a freaky-looking wooden mask. When he held it in front of his face, he looked like a dead-eyed, snaggle-toothed monster in banker's clothing.

A chill tiptoed down my back.

"Art like this is the key to understanding the link between our world and the next," he said. "And that is why it is so important."

Benny nudged me. When I leaned closer, his whispered words tickled my ear. "I bet this guy knows a thing or two about shapeshifters."

I gulped and nodded.

Almost as if he'd heard us, Mr. Sharkawy lifted a jackal

mask from the case and told us about shamans who could turn themselves into animals. He quickly moved on to talking about the other objects, and about how fascinating the museum's exhibit was, and how the installation was nearly finished, and blah, blah, blah.

But Benny and I had heard enough.

When the museum guy closed by saying, "And I hope to see all of you soon—even before the grand opening of our exhibit: *African Art and the Supernatural*," Benny and I traded a look.

"Count on it," I said.

Chapter Seven

Never Face Bad News on an Empty Stomach

AFTER WE SERVED our detention, Benny busted out his amazing skills of persuasion. Somehow, he sweet-talked his mom into dropping us at the comics store while she took the chickens and the rest of our gear home. (For the record, *my* mom would never do something like that unless my little sister, Veronica, was involved. She believes in teaching self-reliance—to boys, anyway.)

Mrs. Tamasese was dealing with a rush of high school kids when we got there. Benny and I hung out by the front counter until she spotted us.

"Howzit, boys?" she called, ringing up some X-Men comics for a couple of teen girls. "I got what you were after."

My breath caught. "You did?"

"Yeah, but"—she surveyed the line and the kids pawing through her bins—"give me about fifteen minutes, okay?"

We promised, and I began to head for the shelf where she kept the *Bone* graphic novels, one of my favorite series. But before I'd taken two steps, Benny grabbed my arm.

"Hold up," he said.

"What?"

"This could be really bad news," Benny said.

"True," I said. "So?"

He raised his pointer finger. "So, as my grandpa always says, never face bad news on an empty stomach."

I cocked my head at him. "Would that be your three-hundred-pound grandpa?"

"Grandpa Ira? Yeah, why?"

"I don't think he faces anything on an empty stomach." Then I thought of what Mrs. Tamasese might tell us and added, "But he's got a point."

"Exactly. To the ice cream shop!"

We stepped back outside and tramped down the block. Just as we reached the corner, a person the size of a four-by-four pickup rounded the building and slammed right into me. I staggered into Benny, and we both went down.

"Watch it!" a deep voice barked.

A huge, muscular man towered over us. Dark stubble dotted his strong jaw and shaven head, and he scowled like he was posing for the cover of *Fierce Frowns Monthly*. He was the kind of hombre who'd play Evil Special Ops Guy in an action movie.

"S-sorry," I said. "I didn't see you."

"Rotten kids," he growled, eyes sizzling. "Tearing around town, causing trouble."

Benny and I picked ourselves up off the sidewalk. "Easy, mister," said Benny. "It was an accident."

I looked up. And up, and up—*hijo*, this guy was big. "We're really, really sorry," I squeaked. "Did I mention that?"

Up close, an animal odor rolled off him like the stink from a dog kennel. I'm no expert, but at a guess, the guy had last taken a bath when Kennedy was president. I tried to breathe through my mouth so my nostrils wouldn't die.

"Someone should teach you kids a lesson," he rumbled. That comment hung in the musky air like a threat. Then, without another word, the giant pushed past us and continued on his way.

"Charming dude," I said with a tight voice.

Benny gave a shaky laugh. "I can already guess your nickname for him," he said. "Mr. Stenchy Pits?"

"Bingo," I said. "What do you think he does for a living? Spy? Truant officer?"

"Preschool teacher," said Benny.

We dismissed this random Monterrosa weirdness and headed on to the scoop shop. After fortifying ourselves with some frozen, ice-creamy goodness, Benny and I retraced our steps to the comics store. A half block away, we heard our names called.

"Rivera, Brackman! Wait up!"

Tina Green hustled down the sidewalk to catch us.

"Hey, Karate Girl," said Benny. "Break any bricks lately?"

"Only faces," she said, all deadpan. When Benny took a step back, she added, "Nah, I'm just yanking your chain."

"Going for some comics?" I asked.

Tina shook her head. "Listen, we need to talk. Something is seriously wrong with Mr. Chu."

"Uh, yeah." I glanced at Benny. "What is up with him and chickens?"

Crossing her arms, Tina said, "Come on. It's not just his normal strangeness anymore, and I know you guys know something about it."

"Whatever do you mean?" asked Benny. He wore that Innocent Blond Angel expression that his mom fell for nearly every time. But not Tina.

"Come off it, Brackman," she said. "Do I look like a mountaintop?"

"Uh, no," he said.

"Then stop trying to snow me. Nobody picks exorcism for their social studies project. I saw how you guys were acting."

I lifted a shoulder. "What? Same as ever."

Tina's eyes narrowed. "You're a terrible liar, Rivera. You guys were hoping all that mumbo jumbo would do something to him, weren't you?"

She was right; I am a terrible liar. I looked to Benny for help.

"Um, we never . . ." he began, until her stare made him squirm. "Oh, all right. Yes, there is something wrong with Mr. Chu."

"What is it?" she asked. "Is he possessed?"

"We don't know for sure," Benny said, glancing up and down the street. "But don't worry. We've got this under control."

Tina barked out a laugh.

"Okay, we're working on it," I said. "Look, you can't tell anybody."

"Why not?" said Tina. "It's obvious to anyone with half a brain. Even Big Pete could tell."

Benny held up his palms in a calming gesture. "We don't want the whole class freaking out," he said.

She snorted. "Oh, like nobody noticed that he tried to munch a live chicken? Get real."

"All right," I said. "We don't want them getting *more* freaked-out."

What I didn't mention was: Benny and I kind of wanted to solve this on our own. After all, we were nobody special—just regular, comics-nerd-type kids. Neither of us had ever done anything big.

Neither of us had ever been the hero before.

Planting her hands on her hips, Tina said, "Stop messing around. This situation calls for serious measures."

"What?" said Benny. "We're serious."

"Sure you are, Chicken Boy. I'm gonna get help from someone who really knows their stuff."

"Who?" I asked.

"Our pastor," she said. "I bet *he* can exorcise evil spirits and get it right."

"Fine," snapped Benny. "Go ahead."

"Fine," said Tina, "I will. This isn't just your problem, you know. It's everyone's problem."

We didn't have an answer for that, so Karate Girl spun and marched off down the street.

"She's right," I said.

"Maybe," said Benny. "But we started trying to cure him first. And we're the ones who are gonna finish it. Come on!"

He hustled into the comics store with me hot on his heels.

Inside, the after-school rush had died down. A few older kids browsed through the bins, but Mrs. Tamasese sat alone at the counter. When she saw us enter, she snagged a slim book from the shelf behind her, jerked her head for us to follow, and wheeled her way over to an unoccupied corner.

Benny and I joined her.

"Well?" he said. "What did you find out?"

Mrs. Tamasese's normally twinkly brown eyes were grave and thoughtful. "It's not good."

Benny's expression told me he was glad we'd had the ice cream.

"Go on," I said.

"First, let me ask if your teacher was still acting weird today. I'm hoping there's another explanation."

We told her about our botched exorcism and Mr. Chu's

increasingly strange behavior. "And he practically mauled Tina to get at that chicken," I finished up.

Mrs. Tamasese's beefy shoulders bunched and she wagged her head ruefully. "Shoots. It's as bad as I thought."

I leaned forward. "What is?"

"What you said about the laughing tipped me off. According to this"—she tapped the book on her lap—"your teacher is becoming . . . a were-hyena."

Benny and I had the exact same reaction. Our eyes goggled, our mouths fell open, and together we said, "A were-*what*?"

Chapter Eight

Hop on Chop

"**A WERE-HYENA,**" Mrs. Tamasese repeated. "I'm almost positive."

"Yeah, right," said Benny, half grinning.

"You're kidding," I said. Mrs. T often talked as though Batman and the Hulk were neighbors of hers. This had to be more of the same.

She didn't crack a smile. "I'm as serious as a choke hold."

"But a were-hyena, in Monterrosa?" I asked. "How is that even possible?"

Benny spread his arms. "Yeah, last I checked, the total hyena population in this part of central California was, like, zero."

The store owner raised a palm, acknowledging our objections. "I know," she said. "Usually, were-critters show up where the real animal lives. Were-jaguars in South

America, were-bears in Norway, were-mongooses—"

"Were-*mongooses?*" said Benny.

"Shouldn't it be were-mongeese?" I asked.

"—in India," Mrs. Tamasese finished. "I don't know why a supernatural creature from Africa would turn up here."

"Maybe it likes the weather?" said Benny.

I raked my fingers through my hair. "Okay, so forget about the why. Our teacher is turning into a were-hyena. What can we do about it?"

"That's the spirit," said Mrs. Tamasese with a tight grin. "Don't back away from a fight."

Something told me she'd never backed away from one in her life.

The former wrestler cracked open her book, which looked about two hundred years old, and paged through it until she found the right section. "Here we go. After a victim is bitten, the monster inside them grows stronger by the day—"

"Wait," I said. "Mr. Chu said he was bitten by a weird dog."

"There you go," said Mrs. Tamasese. "Dogs don't get much weirder than a were-hyena. Now, where was I? Ah. The monster inside them grows until . . ." She licked a finger and turned the page.

"Until?" asked Benny, eyes wide.

". . . at the first full moon, it consumes them completely."

I grimaced. "What does that mean?"

"They're toast," said Mrs. Tamasese. "They're full-on monsters, and it's too late to help them."

"So is Mr. Chu already a were-hyena?" asked Benny.

"Not yet," she said, consulting the book. "It says here that the person who's bitten gets worse each day, but they don't go one hundred percent monstroid until the full moon."

"There's still hope?" I asked, standing up straighter.

Mrs. T lifted a shoulder. "A little. Of course, after that first change, the person turns into a were-creature every moon cycle with no muss or fuss. So it's not all bad."

"Forget that," I said. "We're not going to let it get that far."

Benny met my gaze. "No way, nohow," he said.

"When's the next full moon?" I asked him.

Benny shrugged. Mrs. Tamasese said, "The day after tomorrow."

It felt like someone had punched me in the gut. We only had two days to fix our teacher before he became a monster forever? The sheer size of the task overwhelmed me, and I braced myself on a Xena: Warrior Princess display.

When I looked over at Benny, his pale face had gone ashy. "But how do we cure Mr. Chu in time?" he said.

Mrs. Tamasese flipped a few more pages. "Ah, well, this book doesn't have much on that." She closed the dusty old thing.

"Then what are we gonna do?" I'm not ashamed to say I was freaking a little.

Laying a comforting hand on my arm, Mrs. Tamasese said, "First, don't flip out. As we say in the Islands: cool head main thing."

"Easy for you to say," I blurted. "It's not *your* teacher turning into some giggling monster." I took a deep breath, realized I was being a jerk, and said, "Sorry."

"No sweat," said Mrs. Tamasese. "And believe me, as an ex-wrestler, I know about sweat. Anyhow, as I was saying, this one doesn't have much on cures, but I did find something in another old book." She withdrew a folded sheet of paper from the volume on her lap.

"More *books*?" said Benny. "You couldn't learn this stuff twenty times faster on the Internet?"

She made a face. "Stuff like this? It's ancient knowledge. It's never on computers, only in the oldest books." Clearing her throat, Mrs. Tamasese read aloud:

> *"If the creature thou wouldst best*
> *Find its Maker—brave the test*
> *Hang the charm 'round Maker's throat*
> *Or take its head, in one fell stroke."*

Benny and I were silent for a moment after that. "Run that by me again?" he said. "I don't speak thee-thou."

"I think it's saying that the only way to cure Mr. Chu is to find the were-hyena that bit him?" I said.

"That's right," said Mrs. Tamasese.

"And then we hang some thingy-dingy around its neck?" I said.

"Amulet." She smiled. "Either that or chop off its head in one stroke."

I gulped.

"Classic way to kill a monster," chirped Mrs. Tamasese.

Benny chuckled weakly. "Heh. Better than a silver bullet?"

"For reals." The store owner drew a finger across her neck. "It's the most permanent solution."

My stomach gave a flutter. "There's gotta be another way."

"Not that I could find," said Mrs. Tamasese.

Dang. I sincerely hoped Benny and I could dig up some safer ideas for curing Mr. Chu, and soon. Otherwise there was an excellent chance that the both of us would end up as hyena chow.

And I really didn't want that. It'd be hard to grow up to be a famous cartoonist from inside a monster's belly. Plus, the whole painful-death bit didn't exactly make me feel like dancing the rumba.

By the look on his face, Benny felt the same way. "I'm not the best one-stroke chopper-upper of things," he said. "It took me a whole week to hack up that dead limb that fell in our yard."

"And that was with me helping," I added.

"Then if I were you, I'd go for the amulet," said Mrs. Tamasese.

I raised a hand. "Um, two questions."

"Shoot."

"First, how do we figure out what bit Mr. Chu?"

"Or *who*," said the store owner. "Remember, the were-hyena is a person when the moon isn't full."

Benny threw up his hands. "Great. That's even harder. How do we tell who the monster is when it doesn't look like a monster?"

Mrs. Tamasese shrugged her broad shoulders. "Beats me. It's probably someone who's new in town or who travels. Maybe Mr. Chu can give you some clues."

Not the answer I wanted, but oh, well. "Second, where do we find this amulet?"

Benny gave a hopeful smile. "You got one stashed behind the counter?"

"Sorry, boys," said Mrs. Tamasese. "I'm a shopkeeper, not a witch. Comics sell way better than magic trinkets. Not that comics sell that well. . . ."

I waved my hands around. "So, what? We just look for an Amulets 'n' Things store at the mall and pick out something we like?"

She consulted her sheet of paper again. "Not quite. This book says that the talismans usually come from the same culture as the were-animal."

"So . . . Africa?" Benny's shoulders slumped. "I haven't checked my piggy bank in a while, but I'm pretty sure I can't cover a plane ticket."

A nasal voice cut into our discussion. "Excuse me? I'd like to pay now, if that's all right with you?" A Goth-looking older girl with enough rings in her face to start a jewelry store was tapping her foot impatiently.

"Duty calls," said Mrs. Tamasese. She spun her chair around, then cast a glance over her shoulder. "Good luck, guys. Keep me posted; I'll help however I can."

And with three pumps of those mighty arms, she wheeled away.

Benny and I stumbled out of the store into the weak afternoon sunlight. Cars passed with music blaring. Down the sidewalk, two old ladies laughed at some joke and clutched each other's arm. Life went on around us, but it felt like we were under a giant bubble.

"Maybe we should call the cops," I mumbled. "But what would we tell them? They'd never believe us. . . ."

Plus we'd miss out on our chance to do something heroic for once.

My comment went right past Benny. "What would you use to cut off a were-hyena's head, anyway?" he said, in a dazed voice. "A chain saw? My dad won't even let me stand near him when he's using one."

A thought tickled my mind, but my mind was still too stunned to process it. We shuffled aimlessly down the sidewalk.

"A hacksaw?" Benny asked. "Nah, it'd take too long. An ax?"

The thought kept nagging, but I couldn't hear it over Benny's chatter.

"Or maybe one of those samurai swords," said Benny. "But we'd have to stand on something to get high enough to cut—"

"Stop!" I snapped.

Benny's mouth closed, and his eyes got big. "What'd I say?"

"Just be quiet for one minute and let me think, okay?"

"Okay, okay," said Benny. "Sheesh."

I took a deep breath and let my thoughts roam. Africa . . . amulets . . . hyenas . . . culture of origin . . . Suddenly my brain fog cleared. I clapped a hand to my skull. "I've got it!" I cried.

"What, a case of head lice?" said Benny.

"No, the best place to find African amulets."

Benny frowned. But then, a grin burst out on his face as understanding dawned. "You don't mean . . . ?"

"The museum," we said together.

"Jinx!" we said together.

"Double jinx!"

"Stop it," we both said.

"Triple jinx!"

I put a finger to my lips and Benny echoed the gesture. Then, without another word, we went off to get some culture.

Great White Sharkawy

A S GRAND and impressive as my great-aunt Yolanda, Monterrosa's Museum of Arts and Culture stands at the other end of Main Street. It's just across from the library and two doors down from a doctor who helps with cases of head lice. (Not that I knew anything about that.)

My mom says it's a pretty big museum for such a small town. Of course, she *would* say that; she volunteers there. Benny and I marched up the steps between two massive sculptures of griffins—those mythological creatures with a lion's body and an eagle's head and wings.

Normally, I thought griffins were pretty cool. But that day, I shivered as we passed. It's one thing to think of monsters as resting safely between the pages of a book or up on the TV screen.

But it's a whole other ball game when you learn that monsters are real.

We pushed open the heavy glass doors and stepped into a lobby that felt colder than an Eskimo's icebox. Goose pimples sprouted on my arms and the musty smell of really old things filled my nose. The place was as hushed as a tomb.

"Can I help you?" a disembodied voice asked.

Benny and I jumped, looking around with alarm.

"Over here," the voice called.

On the far side of the lobby, behind a curved counter, sat a pleasant-looking woman whose black hair was shot with gray. Her skin, like mine, was toasty brown. She seemed like somebody's mom dressed up for a PTA meeting.

"Uh, hi," said Benny. "Can we talk to Mr. Sharky?"

A dimple appeared in her cheek. "Sharkawy? You must be from the school he visited today."

"That's right," I said, "and it's really important."

"Is this about our new exhibit?" asked the woman. Her clip-on name tag read MS. ICAZA.

"Well . . . kinda," I said. She seemed like a nice lady, and I didn't want to spook her with the whole shapeshifter thing.

"You know, we went all the way to Africa to select the pieces," said Ms. Icaza.

"That's a lot of frequent flier miles," said Benny. "So, can we see him?"

Her soft face took on a sympathetic expression. "Sorry, boys; he's awfully busy. But you can still check out the exhibit, even though it's not quite finished."

Leaning on the desk, Benny worked his charm. "Pleeease?" he begged. "It's a matter of life and death."

"And we only need five minutes," I added. We both gave her the Bambi eyes.

Ms. Icaza tilted back in her chair and scanned us up and down, chewing the eraser end of her pencil. "Well . . . okay, I'll ask him."

"Thanks a bunch!" chirped Benny.

"But I'm not promising anything." She gestured for us to wait on a nearby bench, and then punched the buttons on her phone pad. Neither of us could relax enough to sit down, so we hovered about. After a brief, muted conversation, Ms. Icaza hung up the phone.

"So?" asked Benny.

"Since it's a matter of life and death," she said, making it clear she didn't entirely believe us, "five minutes."

"Thanks," I said. "This means a lot. Really."

With another dimpled smile, Ms. Icaza rose and crooked a finger, inviting us to follow. We passed through an ebony side door and up a flight of stairs. All the way, she kept up light conversation, asking our names, our grade, and what we thought of the assembly.

Our answers must have pleased her, because she led us down a short corridor and rapped on the door that read MUSEUM DIRECTOR. "Mr. Sharkawy?" she called. A muffled voice answered, and Ms. Icaza opened the door, ushering us through.

In the middle of a room decorated with exotic statues and carved masks squatted a gleaming wooden desk the size of a battleship. Behind that desk, his back as straight as an admiral, sat Mr. Helmet Hair himself—the man from our assembly, Mr. Sharkawy. If possible, his hair shone even more than his desktop.

Now he turned his piercing eyes on us. "I'm not in the habit of granting random interviews," he said. "Is this for your school newspaper?"

"Not exactly," I said.

"We need your help," blurted Benny, "with our teach—" I nudged him. "With a *report* for our teacher," he said.

"And you can't get that by viewing our exhibits?" The man's gaze dropped to some papers on his desk.

"No!" Benny and I said together.

"Please, sir, we need to ask you some questions about . . ." I faltered.

His "Yes?" sounded bored. Mr. Sharkawy picked up a pen and jotted a note.

We were losing him.

Benny jumped in. "It's about shapeshifters."

I winced, but I was glad Benny said it first. Even though

I was seriously worried about Mr. Chu, I felt foolish discussing this supernatural stuff with any grown-up other than Mrs. Tamasese.

The man's eyebrows lifted.

I braced for laughter, saying, "Not that we really believe in them, but . . ."

The museum director put down his pen. "And why not? There used to be much less separation between humans and animals, between the normal and the numinous."

Benny's forehead scrunched up. "Numinous?"

"The world of spirit," said Mr. Sharkawy with an elegant twist of his hand. "Our ancestors believed that people could change into animals; why do we find that so hard to swallow today?"

Benny and I shrugged.

"What's your interest in shapeshifters?" asked Ms. Icaza from the doorway. I'd forgotten she was there.

"Oh, uh . . ." I said, turning. "We . . ."

"We think they're cool," said Benny.

With a these-kids-are-cuckoo smile, Ms. Icaza closed the door and left us with Mr. Sharkawy. His dark eyes sparkled. "Well, I think they're 'cool,' too," he said. You got the feeling that the word had never crossed his lips before that moment. "What would you like to know?"

Benny and I traded a glance. If the museum director thought shapeshifters were awesome, we couldn't very well start out by asking him how to break the curse.

"How do people get the ability to change?" I asked.

"It's quite fascinating, really," said Mr. Sharkawy, leaning back and lacing his fingers behind his head. "Some use potions or magic charms, some wear the actual skin of the animal . . ."

"Ugh," said Benny. I shot him a look, and he lost his disgusted expression in a hurry.

"And some tribal shamans invite animal possession through rituals," the museum director continued.

"What about . . . biting?" I asked.

Nodding, Mr. Sharkawy said, "Certainly, if one is bitten by a shapeshifter—the blessed bite—one can gain the gift of transformation."

Blessed bite? Benny mouthed at me.

"That *is* fascinating," I said, laying it on thick. "And what if someone wanted to cure himself?"

"Cure himself?" The man's thick eyebrows drew together like two gypsy moths colliding, and he leaned forward aggressively. "Why on earth would anyone reject the dark gift?"

"Yeah," said Benny, jumping on board. "Why would they?"

I sent him a quick glare. "Well, maybe they got it by accident and didn't really want it."

In a flash, Mr. Sharkawy stood, looming over us. "Only a fool would turn down that kind of power."

Whoa. Benny and I took a step back. Clearly this guy

took his shapeshifting seriously. "Well, sure," said Benny. "He'd have to be nuts. A total wacko. But just out of curiosity—for our report—how would he break the curse?"

"Curse?" Thunder boomed in the man's voice, and he stalked around the desk. "*Curse?* That's precisely the kind of wrongheaded thinking I've been fighting against."

We edged backward. "Of course it is," I said. "And we'd never ever use a word like that in our report, would we, Benny?"

"Never ever." Benny shook his head. "But *if* some misguided person was looking for a so-called cure . . ."

Mr. Sharkawy was on top of us in three long strides. He clapped his hands onto our shoulders and spun us around. "Come with me," he ordered.

"I, uh," I stammered as he propelled us toward a side door. Adrenaline pumped through me as my imagination kicked into hyperdrive. Where was he taking us? Some kind of museum jail for rude boys? A pit full of hungry alligators? Or would we become a sacrifice for some twisted beast he had chained up behind the door?

"Open it," snapped the museum director. Gingerly, Benny turned the doorknob.

The man thrust us ahead of him down a narrow corridor, which soon opened into a display room. Now we stood in the museum proper, surrounded by creepy-cool African masks, sculptures, and carvings—all lit dramatically like props in some big-budget horror movie. A snarling lion head carved in wood made my skin crawl.

"Look!" demanded Mr. Sharkawy. "Look at the care and the artistry these long-ago people poured into their craft."

"Nice," I said.

"They spent all this effort to cause a supernatural transformation into a higher state, and all you want to know is how to reverse it?" The museum director practically snarled. His nose sliced the air like a hawk's beak.

"Um, yeah?" said Benny. "Just for our report."

"Others believed like you," Mr. Sharkawy said. "Fools. Those who feared the raw power of our animal selves."

"Can't imagine why," I said, thinking of our teacher's increasingly out-of-control behavior, his cruelty. And this museum guy wasn't looking too stable himself. Could he be somehow mixed up with the were-hyenas?

"Behold the craftsmanship on this Edo mask," the man continued. "Exquisite detail, yes? And this stork-headed Yoruba staff—quite remarkable."

My eyes slid past the objects to some necklaces hanging on the wall in an unfinished part of the exhibit. "What about those?" I asked.

Making a dismissive wave, Mr. Sharkawy scoffed, "Those fools I mentioned, they wore amulets like these to bring the change back under control. Ridiculous! Wasteful!"

Amulets?

While Benny murmured an agreement to Mr. Looney Tunes, I took a closer peek at the necklaces. Several featured a pendant shaped like the head of an animal. I spotted a leopard, a lion, a crocodile, and something doglike—a hyena?

My eyes sought Benny's. Could this be what we were after? He saw where I'd been looking and drifted nearer.

"Hey," Benny said, "is that—?" His hand reached out toward the amulet with the doglike head.

"Don't touch!" Mr. Sharkawy boomed, swatting Benny's hand away. "Those are priceless. What on earth were you thinking?"

"I just—" Benny began.

Fingers like talons clamped down on Benny's shoulder and mine. "I made a mistake," said Mr. Sharkawy in a tight voice. "I thought that you . . . children might appreciate something this special, but clearly I was wrong."

He steered us through the exhibit toward a nearby elevator, moving so fast that I stumbled over my own feet.

"We *do* appreciate it," I said. "You've been a big help."

"More than you know," Benny added.

Unyielding, Mr. Sharkawy dragged us to the elevator door and mashed the button with his thumb like he was squashing a bug. "You will leave now," he said. "You're not ready for sacred mysteries."

When the door slid open, he shoved us inside and stabbed the first-floor button. We rode down together in silence. As Mr. Sharkawy hauled us across the lobby, Ms. Icaza called cheerily from behind her desk, "Good-bye, boys! Come again anytime."

Holding open the heavy glass door so we had to squeeze past him, the museum director muttered, "Don't you dare." Beneath his overpowering citrus-y aftershave, I caught a sharp, musky scent. Mr. Sharkawy smelled nearly as funky as the big dude we'd bumped into by the comics store.

Were grown-ups experiencing a serious deodorant shortage, or was there another, darker explanation?

The door shut, then locked behind us with a hard click. Benny and I stood on the steps, blinking in the late afternoon sunshine.

"Can you believe that wacko?" said Benny.

"Him and his 'dark gift,'" I said. "I'd hate to see what's under his Christmas tree."

Benny leaned closer. "Was that necklace what I think it was?"

"A big break for us," I said. Glancing over my shoulder, I caught Mr. Sharkawy's suspicious glare burning a hole through the glass door. "Uh, maybe we should go somewhere and talk."

Benny lifted his pointer finger. "To the tree house, Robin!" he said.

"Wait, how come I never get to be Batman?"

He shrugged. "Because I've always been battier than you?"

"Can't argue with that," I said. "Let's go."

Chapter Ten

The Tree Stooges

EVERY DYNAMIC DUO needs a clubhouse. Benny and I were no exception. The vacant lot between his house and mine grew in a wild tangle, choked with tall grass, shaggy bushes, and three gnarled oak trees. In the biggest of those trees, someone long gone had built a sturdy platform with a railing and no roof.

Ever since we'd been old enough to scale the twisted trunk, Benny and I had used that tree fort in countless games of spies, and army, and Lord of the Rings.

Now we retreated there to make plans and drink sodas. (Sodas from my house, not Benny's. His mom only lets them have juice or healthy drinks that taste like Odor-Eaters and brewed bark.)

"Abuelita gave me a half hour," I said as we got settled. "Then I have to do homework before dinner."

"So let's make it snappy," said Benny. He took a long slurp from his can and let out an impressive burp.

I made a "not bad" face, chugged my drink, and ripped out a belch of my own, just as loud.

He nodded. "This meeting is officially called to order. First, let me ask the obvious: How weird is it that we've got a were-hyena problem in Monterrosa?"

"Deeply weird," I said.

"I mean, how would something like that even get here?" he asked.

I shrugged. "On vacation? As a stowaway? Ooh, maybe that Sharkawy guy smuggled it in his luggage."

Benny hunched forward. "Or maybe *he's* the were-hyena."

"Maybe he is. He sure smells like a hyena cage—did you get a whiff of his armpits?"

He fanned the air in front of his face. "Seriously stenchy."

"But whoever the creature is," I said, "what are the odds that it would bite Mr. Chu?"

It was Benny's turn to shrug. "Beats me. I'm not doing so hot in math."

I blew out a long sigh. "I'm worried about him. Mrs. T said he won't be a full-on hyena until tomorrow night—"

"Yikes," Benny interrupted with a shudder.

"But what if he accidentally hurts someone—or himself—before then?"

We stared at each other, struck by how little time we had to save our teacher, and how woefully unprepared we were for the job. Did all wannabe heroes feel like this?

Benny shook his head to clear it. "Look, the way I see it, we've got two ways to attack the problem."

Leaning back against the tree trunk, I said, "Lay 'em on me."

"Either we start by going after the amulet, or by finding the were-hyena that bit Mr. Chu."

"Makes sense," I said. "But then we've got to get both of them, or the cure won't work, and—"

"Bye-bye, Mr. Chu," he finished.

We fell silent for a moment, thinking about the possibility of losing our favorite teacher. At least *I* was thinking that—Benny may have been thinking about chugging another soda and burping "The Star-Spangled Banner," for all I knew.

"Just a few minor challenges that I can see," I said.

It was Benny's turn to lean back. "Lay 'em on me."

"First, the amulet—if that's even the one we need—is kept in a locked building protected by alarms."

"Yup," said Benny.

"Second, I'm not a spy with mad lockpicking skills, and last I checked, neither were you."

"True," said Benny.

"And third," I continued, "we have absolutely no clue who the were-hyena is when it's not a were-hyena."

He shook his head, frowning. "Those are problems, all right. We need a good solution." Suddenly Benny's eyes widened. "Oh!"

"A solution?" I said hopefully.

"A splinter." He twisted onto one hip and plucked at his jeans.

I rolled my eyes.

"But no worries," said Benny. A grin teased his lips, and he sat up straighter. "I'm about to be brilliant."

I snorted. "And everyone said that day would never come."

Leaning toward me, Benny said, "Maybe it's hard to figure out who the were-hyena is during the day . . ."

"Try almost impossible," I said. "It could be anyone."

"But at night . . ." His eyebrows lifted and his hands spread as he waited for me to complete his thought.

"At night, it's a savage, crazed were-hyena. Duh. So?"

"So that's the time to catch it." He crossed his arms.

Gaping at Benny like he'd sprouted giant bug antennae, I sat speechless. At last, I stuttered, "C-Catch it?"

"Yeah." Benny scooted closer, taken by his idea. "Can't be more than one or two were-hyenas in Monterrosa, see? So it's quicker to find Mr. Chu's maker at night than spend all day trying the amulet on everybody in town."

"You're serious," I said.

"Of course." He rubbed his hands together. "Mr. Chu said he got bitten out by the graveyard, right?"

"Right."

Benny stood, acting out his plan. "So we find that trap my dad got back when that black bear was running loose, we set it up by the graveyard, and we catch the were-hyena. *Bam!* Problem solved."

Climbing to my feet, I said, "That's the craziest thing I've ever heard."

"That's why it'll work."

I clapped both hands onto my head to keep my brain from exploding. "But . . ." I spluttered. "You . . . we . . ."

Holding up his palm like a traffic cop, Benny said, "I know, you're wondering what we'll use for bait. Any raw meat should do the trick—hamburger, chicken, whatever. Hyenas aren't picky."

From across the field, my grandma called, "Caaarrlos! Come hooome!" She stood at our back gate, waving.

I waved back. "Coming!" To Benny, I said, "Forget bait. Do you know how dangerous that monster is? What's to stop it from skipping the hamburger and going straight for the Benny-and-Carlos special?"

"No worries. We set the trap near a tree, so we'll have a quick getaway. Everyone knows hyenas can't climb trees."

"But—"

Benny shrugged. "It's the simplest way."

"Yeah, but simple doesn't mean easy," I said.

He scoffed. "We catch it tonight; we steal the amulet tomorrow. Slip it over the person's head before the moon comes up, and—*bam!*—we get our teacher back."

I frowned. "You know, saying 'bam' doesn't make this plan any safer."

"I know," said Benny, "but I like saying 'bam.'" His eyebrows raised. "Got any better ideas?"

"Caaarrlos!" my grandma called again. *"¡Ven aca!"*

Through gritted teeth, I told him, "Not yet."

As we climbed down from the tree house, Benny said, "Great. Gear up and I'll meet you back here tonight at ten thirty."

"Great," I echoed. But what I really meant was *¡ay, huey!*

I had so much on my mind at dinner, I almost missed the clues that my dad had something on *his* mind. He sighed. He toyed with his food. But I didn't take much note of it. While chewing my grandma's spicy meat loaf, I kept chewing over other ways for Benny and me to cure our teacher—always coming up short.

Not even Zeppo's shaggy head on my lap could break my distracted mood. (Of course, he was just there for any scraps that fell.)

Finally, as we were tucking into our vanilla ice cream, my dad cleared his throat. "Carlos, I heard from your mom today."

"Huh?" I'd been weighing the pros and cons of finding the were-hyena by dragging roadkill through downtown and seeing if anyone tried to eat it.

"Your mother. She called." His face was frowny, not smiley like it should've been if the news was good.

I slurped a spoonful of my ice cream. "Veronica didn't get the part?"

Abuelita and he exchanged a significant look.

"Well . . ." she said.

"What?" I said.

My dad set down his spoon. "No, *chámaco*, she did. Your sister scored a supporting role on a Disney Channel show."

"Wow, that's terrific!" I was genuinely happy for my little sister, even if she was a total brat. She'd wanted to act ever since she was four and first understood that Jessie Prescott wasn't a real person.

Of course, that didn't mean that I didn't feel a stab of jealousy at all the attention Veronica was getting.

Dad looked down, running his finger over a seam in the tablecloth. "It *is* terrific, son. She's turning cartwheels. Literally. But here's the thing."

Uh-oh. There was some kind of catch. It felt like the ice cream had frozen my innards. "We're not moving to L.A., are we?"

My dad tilted his head. "Not exactly."

"We *can't* leave Monterrosa, Dad. Not now." What would happen to Mr. Chu if we did? Would he and his maker bite everyone and populate the town with monsters?

"Don't worry, mijo." My grandma reached across the table and patted my hand. "You look so serious."

Dad sighed some more. "*We're* not moving to L.A. Your mom and sister are."

"Oh."

And here I'd thought nothing could distract me from the threat of my teacher becoming a were-hyena.

Chapter Eleven

Fright-Eyed and Bushy-Tailed

ONE ADVANTAGE of having a lot to worry about is you don't have to worry about falling asleep before a late-night adventure. Instead of dozing off, I sneaked a few things into an old Donald Duck fanny pack—a flashlight, a whistle, some bug spray, two strips of beef jerky, a fist-sized hunk of hamburger, and a Snickers bar. It didn't exactly look cool, but it would do the job.

Then I waited for the house to get quiet.

By ten forty-five, all I could hear was faint snoring from my dad down the hall. Abuelita had gone home to her condo, so the coast was clear. Moving as quietly as a ninja tiptoeing on velvet, I boosted up my bedroom window and slipped into the night.

A swollen moon leered from behind the clouds. One more night, and it'd be full. As I passed near the back door, a faint whining came from behind it. Zeppo.

"Shh!" I hissed.

He whimpered louder. Glancing at my dad's window, I saw it was still dark. But it wouldn't stay that way if Zeppo kept this up.

Pulling out my key, I unlocked the back door and tossed in one of the beef jerky strips. I heard the sound of scrabbling paws, then chewing.

Before Zeppo could get amped up again, I relocked the door and hurried across the yard. The air was as cool and crisp as celery straight from the fridge. A faint smell of woodsmoke and eucalyptus leaves teased my nose.

I opened the gate as slowly as possible, clenching my teeth and freezing in my tracks whenever it creaked. The house stayed dark, so I slipped through and closed the gate. Shielding the flashlight beam with my fingers, I followed its faint path through the bushes to the tree house.

"You're late," Benny hissed from the shadows.

"I know," I whispered. "I'll tell you why later."

He hefted a knapsack of hyena-trapping supplies onto his back and gave me a thumbs-up.

Creeping along single file, we followed a path that wound through the tall weeds, among the trees, and out onto a side street. Everything was hushed, dead still. No cars approached.

Once we hit the sidewalk, we uncovered our flashlights and I caught Benny up on the news at my house.

"Wow," he said. "So you won't see your mom and sister at all?"

"Only on weekends," I said. "They'll stay in L.A. during the week."

Benny's grin gleamed white in the moonlight. "Hey, you'll be like an only child. Wish I could be one. Got any bright ideas about getting rid of my brother and sister?"

"Ha ha," I said. "This is serious. What if my mom decides she *likes* living there? What if she and my dad get . . ." I couldn't say it.

"Divorced?" said Benny.

"Well . . . yeah."

He flapped a hand. "Never happen."

"It happened with Tyler Spork's parents. His mom got a job in San Francisco and never came back." My gut gave a nervous twist.

"She never came back because Tyler's a major doo-doo-head," said Benny.

I considered, and felt a little better. "Well, there is that."

What I didn't confess to Benny was my envy. I mean, what guy gets jealous of his baby sister? But Veronica was on her way to stardom, and I was just a regular, boring kid. I felt a burning in my belly, hotter than jalapeño salsa. I needed to show my parents that I could be special, too.

Did Benny feel the same way?

We took the shortcut across the Little League diamonds. Washed silver by moonlight, they were as empty as blank sheets of paper. The metal thingy on the rope *ting-ting*-ed against the flagpole. A lonely sound.

Neither of us had dared to try sneaking out our bikes, so we had a long walk ahead. Down a deserted Main Street, left on Duffett Avenue, and up Oswald Road we went, heading for the graveyard. The houses stood farther and farther apart as we hiked onward. Finally, we reached a stretch of road bordered only by wild land.

Most of the way, Benny kept up a running commentary. But as we drew closer to our destination, even he fell silent.

At the turnoff to the cemetery, we paused. Our eyes met. This was it.

It felt like a hive of bees was having a fiesta in my chest. From the knees up, I jittered and twitched. But my feet stayed planted.

Somewhere in the dark woods beside the road, a twig snapped. We both jumped. After a breathless minute when nothing else moved, we relaxed. A little.

"So . . ." said Benny.

"So . . ." I said.

"Here we go."

"Yup. Here we go."

We stood there for another minute.

"Just a quick in and out," said Benny.

"Yup, just plant the trap and go."

I took a deep breath, and then a step, followed by another. Benny matched me, stride for stride. As we scanned the darkness, our heads swiveled like a mambo dancer's hips.

The graveyard access road coiled onward, a strip of lighter gray in the charcoal gray of the woods. No streetlamps lit its length. Much like our plan, our flashlights seemed pitifully inadequate.

The night held its breath. A strange bird called. Trees rustled like shrouds in the soft breeze. The smell of freshly turned earth rose around us, full and rich and dirt-y.

When I splashed my flashlight beam across the grounds, it revealed tombstones tilting like lines of LEGOs sinking in a swamp. Nearest the road, one grave looked half-dug, with soil piled randomly around it, almost like the mess Zeppo made when he was trying to find an old bone.

Benny spotted the heap. "What's that?"

I lifted a shoulder. "Dunno. Maybe they didn't finish yet?"

He added his light to mine and approached the grave. Trailing behind him, I said, "Um, shouldn't we stay on the road?"

"It may be a clue," said Benny.

"You've been watching too much *Scooby-Doo*."

His flashlight picked out an odd bundle of cloth on the far side of the grave mound. It looked like the shape lay half in, half out of the hole.

"What the . . . ?" Benny said.

At the exact same moment, we both froze. We recognized the shape for what it was: a fresh corpse, dragged from the ground, half stripped of its clothing, and partially eaten.

¡Dios mio! A wave of horror and nausea rushed through me. I couldn't seem to catch my breath.

"It's a . . . dead body!" I wheezed.

"And something's been munching on it!" Benny gasped.

When I gulped, I could taste spicy meat loaf in the back of my throat.

Benny's fists clenched, and he swayed, shoulders up around his ears. He was babbling something under his breath that sounded like "Don't scream, don't scream, don't scream."

All of a sudden the potent cocktail of dread and disgust proved too much for me. I hunched over, hands on knees, and lost my dinner and dessert.

Benny was so overcome by the sight of the corpse, he didn't even razz me about my ralphing. He stayed rooted in place, staring and rocking back and forth.

After a moment or two, I wiped my mouth. Keeping my gaze away from the dead body, I grabbed Benny's arm. "Come on." Half-dazed, he didn't resist.

We sidled back toward the road, sweeping our flashlights from side to side so that whatever had done the munching couldn't sneak up on us. My imagination supplied zombies, wild dogs, and yes, great big were-hyenas.

"You don't suppose a . . ." I began.

At that moment, a high, screaming laugh shattered the cemetery's peace.

Eeeee-huh-huh-huh-huh!

". . . were-hyena dug that up?" said Benny. "Oh, yeah."

My free hand fumbled with his book bag. "Quick, the trap!"

"Let me!" he said, trying to slip it off his shoulders.

For a few seconds, we fought each other, fingers clumsy with panic. My heart thudded like a jackhammer. Finally, we tore open his bag and removed the heavy bear trap.

"Help me!" Benny whispered, setting the sinister device on the ground. Its heavy jaws were closed, and two long springs on either side were held in place by clamps. A thick, yard-long chain ran from the trap to a steel hoop.

"What do I do?" I asked, scanning the cemetery for signs of movement.

Straining to part the jaws, Benny grunted, "Take one side."

Together, we managed to spread the two halves of the trap until it clicked open. Its wicked teeth glinted in the flashlight beam.

"Now the bait," said Benny.

I groped through my fanny pack and dug out the chunk of hamburger. Unwrapping the tinfoil, I hesitated. "But— how do I put it on the pan without losing a hand?"

"Here," said Benny. "You—"

Eeeee-huh-huh-huh-huh!

That maniacal laugh rang out again, even closer. Ice water squirted through my veins. We swung our flashlights about wildly, trying to spot the creature. No luck. A sturdy oak tree grew about fifteen feet away, and I was tempted to climb it immediately.

Snatching the hamburger off my palm, Benny plopped it onto the pan in the trap's center. "It's not active until you take these off." He fumbled with one spring's clip, and I knelt to remove the other.

"Hurry!" I said.

And then, a low rumbling from behind us made all my muscles tighten like the steel spring in my hands. My breath stopped. My legs shook like maracas. My mouth went dryer than a Death Valley Triscuit.

Slowly, stiffly, I swiveled my head. What I saw on the road turned my insides to melted mozzarella.

Chapter Twelve

Scare Package

THE CREATURE towered well over six feet tall. Roughly man-shaped, its proportions were all wrong, with too-long arms and a too-big head. And what a head! That face, straight out of nightmares, with mad little eyes, batlike ears, and a wet snarling mouth that put me in mind of a great white shark—all fangs and hunger.

A string of drool dangled from that mouth, glistening in the moonlight.

"Nngh!" said Benny.

"Guh," I agreed.

My hands trembled so badly I managed to pull the clip off the spring completely by accident. Ever so slowly, I rose into a half crouch, stopping when the beast growled again.

Someone whose voice sounded like a terrified Mickey Mouse said, "Let's go!" I think it might have been me.

"A-a-almost done," said Benny.

I gulped. "*Now*, Benny! We're standing between it and the hamburger."

The nightmare figure advanced a step. I edged away from the trap.

Benny continued to fiddle with it. "N-n-no w-worries," he said. "Hy-yi-yenas are c-c-cowards."

The were-creature roared and unfolded to its full height, brawny arms spread.

Hairs I hadn't even grown yet stood on end like porcupine quills.

"Ix-nay on the oward-cay!" I cried. "It understands English!"

I backed toward the oak tree, never taking my eyes off the were-hyena. Benny joined me. I had no idea whether he'd finished prepping the trap, but at this point we had one or two other things to worry about. Like how to avoid getting eaten.

"N-no sudden moves," I said. "It makes them chase you." I must have picked that up from some nature documentary.

The monster took another step toward us.

We turned and ran, screaming our heads off. (Oh, yeah, like *you* wouldn't have done the same in our shoes.)

Ignoring our neat little trap and its hamburger patty, the were-creature unleashed an unnerving cackle and gave chase. His speed was *amazing*. If we hadn't been four times as close to the tree as he was, we never would've reached it in time.

Up, up, up, we scrambled, gibbering in terror. When we got as high as we could safely climb, we clung to a limb and watched. The massive were-hyena paced back and forth below the tree, chuckling and snarling to itself, as if debating whether we'd taste better plain or with mayonnaise.

After a few minutes of this, either we maxed out on scared-ness or our brains went numb with shock, because Benny and I were able to have a more or less normal conversation. That is, until Benny made his comment about how dumb were-hyenas can't climb trees, and the monster set out to prove him wrong.

It took a running start and leaped up onto the trunk, sinking those sharp claws into the bark like a cat on a scratching post—a really big, homicidal cat. My stomach flipped. Then the monster took one hand off the tree to climb higher and slid back down instead, carving strips into the bark.

"Awww!" Benny taunted. "Poor widdow hyena fall down, go boom."

"Shhh!" I shushed him furiously. "You're making it worse."

Benny grimaced. "Sorry. I got caught up in the moment."

The were-hyena snarled and made another attempt, this time managing to wriggle his way up to eight feet below

our perch. From this distance, his eyes were pits of blackness rimmed with red, and his teeth looked like a set of ivory steak knives, ready to slice. The stink of rotting flesh wafted upward.

The creature wore no shred of clothing, and though some of its actions were human-ish, it could've been anyone from our postman to a total stranger. No way to tell.

Benny broke off a piece of dead branch and hurled it down. It missed by a mile. The monster growled.

"Hit it with something!" cried Benny. "What've we got?" He patted his pockets and peered woefully down at his book bag and flashlight lying on the ground, next to the trap. "I've got zip. You?"

Unlike Benny, I still had both my light and the fanny pack. Carefully, I brought it around onto my lap to take stock. A whistle, a can of bug spray, a piece of beef jerky, and a Snickers bar.

Not exactly an arsenal.

I shook the spray can about a jillion times, held it as low as my arm could reach, and gave it a long blast until it was empty—*ffffsssshhht!* Misty clouds of chemicals billowed out.

Right off, Benny and I began coughing and choking. The were-hyena kept inching upward, undisturbed.

"The wind's—*cough*—blowing the wrong—*hack*—way," I spluttered. I chucked the can at the monster, and it bounced off one beefy shoulder. The creature didn't even blink.

"At least—*hack*—mosquitoes won't bug us while we're being eaten alive," said Benny. "What else you—*cough*—got?"

"The flashlight!"

I clicked it on and shone it directly into the were-hyena's eyes. Instantly, they glowed a spooky shade of green. The monster hissed, whipping its head back and forth to avoid the beam. I followed with the light. Then it simply shut its eyes and kept on inching upward.

"*¡Porque!*" I cried. "Not fair!"

Benny snatched the beef jerky from my bag and waved it about, saying, "Look, Laughing Boy! Din-din!" He pitched it off to the side.

The were-hyena watched the strip fall with a total lack of interest. Its attention returned to us, and I swear, it wore a "Really? That's all you got?" expression on its face.

"Yeah, I'm not crazy about jerky either," muttered Benny. "Carlos, what's left?"

Aside from the whistle and my nearly empty fanny pack itself, only one item remained: my Snickers bar.

Benny reached for it, but I grabbed the candy first.

"Throw it!" he said.

"But what if we're up here all night?" I said. "We might get hungry."

"If he eats us, it won't matter."

Still I resisted. "It's the last of my Halloween stash. Monsters don't like candy."

"But they *do* like fourth-grade boys," said Benny. "Throw it!"

Reluctantly, I unwrapped the candy bar. The were-hyena's ears perked up at the rustling wrapper. After saying a silent good-bye to the treat, I chucked the Snickers away from the tree.

Amazingly, the were-hyena reached for it, missed, and tumbled back down the trunk.

"Shut the front door!" I said.

With a half smile and a shrug, Benny said, "Well, it *is* part human."

After that, the monster abandoned tree climbing. Benny hadn't had time to release the bear trap's second spring, so the were-hyena easily gulped down the hamburger bait, followed by the Snickers bar.

"Aw, man!" said Benny, watching the creature.

"It wouldn't have worked anyway," I said. "We forgot to anchor the trap to anything."

"Aw, man," he repeated. "Monster trapping is so much easier in the movies."

For what felt like a whole Ice Age but may have been only a few hours, the were-hyena prowled about the base of the tree, growling up at us and chuckling insanely. Then we heard a sound:

Eeeee-huh-huh-huh-huh!

Another were-hyena called from across the graveyard! Our monster answered its cry, and they held a brief, eerie conversation. Finally, our creature cast us one last baleful look and loped off into the darkness.

Benny and I sagged against the trunk. My belly slowly unclenched.

"A second were-hyena," I said.

"Yup," said Benny.

"So we don't even know if ours was the one that bit Mr. Chu," I said.

"Nope."

"So all this might have been for nothing?"

"Yup." Benny winced.

A headache throbbed behind my eyes. "What we really need," I said, "is a new plan."

Chapter Thirteen

Karate Girl Jumps In

BY THE TIME Benny and I made it home, yawning and stumbling, the sky was just beginning to lighten in the east. I tumbled through my window and collapsed into bed without even taking off my clothes.

When my dad came in, it felt like I had barely closed my eyes.

"Wake up, sleepyhead," he said, shaking my shoulder.

"Gnnf," I replied, turning over.

Dad whisked the covers back. Seeing I was fully dressed, he said, "You know, there's this new invention called pajamas. You might want to check 'em out."

"Umza mumza," I mumbled.

My tongue was a pulverized sausage, and my eyelids

were stuck together with superglue. When I pried them apart, I saw him standing by my bed in his work uniform: crisp, white long-sleeved shirt, nice slacks, and shiny work shoes. Dad always says computer programmers don't need to dress up, so that's why he does.

"Let's go, buddy," he said. "Your grandma won't be coming over until after school, so I whipped up some breakfast. Let's move it."

I never knew it was possible to shower and eat while asleep, but somehow I managed it. This, I thought, must be why grown-ups drink coffee.

"Come on," said my dad, twirling his car keys around a finger, "I'll drop you and Benny at school."

A few minutes later, as we were waiting for Benny to come out of his house, my dad glanced up from his smartphone. "You know, whenever you want to talk more about what's going on with Veronica and your mom, I'm here."

"Yeah, I know," I said. The window glass felt cool against my forehead.

"It won't be easy—for any of us—but it's your sister's dream come true."

"I know." I stared at Benny's front door.

"We need to be supportive," said my dad, scrubbing a hand over his lower face.

"I'm happy for her," I said. "Really." And I was. But my brain was still stuck on last night's failure in the graveyard— how it hadn't exactly made me a hero, and how if we didn't do something drastic, Mr. Chu would be overtaken by his inner monster tonight.

"Is something else on your mind, buddy?" said my dad.

I bit my lip. Time to do something drastic.

"Yeah," I said. "There is." Then I took a deep breath and proceeded to spill everything about Mr. Chu's curse, about all we'd learned, and about how we were trying to save him.

Benny arrived partway through my tale. During the brief ride to school, he chimed in with details. When we were finished, my dad stopped the car across the street from the school and stared at us, shaking his head.

"Boys," he said, "that's the best Halloween story I've ever heard. But you're a week too late."

"But, Dad, it's not a story!" I said.

He chuckled, reaching across me to open the passenger door. "With your imaginations, you boys should be screenwriters."

"We're telling the truth, Mr. Rivera," said Benny. "Honest. Something's horribly wrong with Mr. Chu, and we have to stop it. Today."

"I'm sure he just caught some kind of bug," said my dad.

My ears grew warm. "You didn't see him attack that chicken," I said. "Or growl, or laugh like a maniac."

He held up a hand. "Maybe your teacher is having trouble at home, and it's made him unstable."

Benny leaned over the back of the front seat. "But we

saw the monster—both of us. How do you explain that?"

Dad gave us an indulgent smile. "Another bear wandered into town. There was something about it in the news."

"But—" I said.

"Now, now. I know how fear can mess with your perceptions."

"But—" said Benny.

A sudden thought struck my father and his expression turned as serious as a daylong dental surgery. "Wait a minute. You really sneaked out to the graveyard last night?"

"We really did," Benny and I said.

"Then you're grounded," he told me. "And you will be," he said to Benny, "as soon as I tell your father."

"No!" I cried. "You can't!"

His black eyes sizzled. "I'm your father; I can do what I like. Now get out of this car and go to school. You're making me late for work."

"Da-a-ad!"

"Carlos . . ."

I opened my mouth to protest again, but what I saw in his face made me think twice. "Okay," I grumbled, climbing out of the car.

Standing at the curb and watching my dad drive away, Benny said, "Grounded? How do we steal an amulet and hang it around some hyena-man's neck if we're grounded?"

"I have no idea," I said, feeling like I'd just been chopped off at the knees.

In a daze we stumbled to class. As Benny and I passed the flagpole, Tina Green was waiting with some more bad news.

"I followed through on our plan," she said, falling in beside us.

"What plan?" I asked.

"Getting my pastor to do an exorcism on Mr. Chu," said Tina.

"Oh," said Benny dully, "*your* plan."

Tina tossed her braids over one shoulder. "At first he didn't believe me. Then he said Lutherans don't really do exorcisms these days. But when I talked him into going to Mr. Chu's house with me to 'counsel' him, things got weird."

I glanced over at her. "What do you mean?"

Tina grimaced. "He was digging through the trash can looking for treats."

"Your pastor?" said Benny.

"Mr. Chu," said Tina, scowling. "When Pastor Wilson tried to talk with him, he kept laughing like a loon and going on about how the woods were his church."

"Okay," I said. "That's only semiweird."

"Right," said Tina. "But then, when Pastor Wilson took out his Bible, Mr. Chu snatched it away and started gnawing on it like a chew toy. He told him he'd never been so insulted in his life."

"Mr. Chu?" said Benny.

"Pastor Wilson," said Tina. "Keep up, Brackman. Anyway, he ended up chasing us away from his house and biting the pastor on the butt."

"Butt biting," I said. "That *is* weird."

"Pastor told me he called a shrink to help out, but Mr. Chu refused to talk to her."

"No surprise there," said Benny.

Tina walked backward so she could look both of us in the eye. "The adults clearly have no clue. It's up to us. What are we going to do about this situation?"

"*We're* not gonna do anything," said Benny gloomily. We trudged down the short hallway that led to our classroom.

Tina scoffed. "Are you still stuck on that us-boys-have-gotta-do-it-alone bullpucky?"

"Worse," I said. "We're grounded."

Rolling her eyes, she said, "And you're going to let a little thing like that stop you?"

"Maybe?" I said.

Tina waved her arms about. "Did the Ghostbusters give up when the city tried to shut them down? Did Robin Hood crawl back into bed when the sheriff put a price on his head?"

"No, but—" Benny began.

But Tina was on a roll. "I say we march into that classroom, roll up our sleeves, and figure out how to turn Mr. Chu back into the teacher we all know and love!"

A faint stirring of hope tickled inside my chest. "Yeah," I said.

"Yeah!" said Benny. "Grounded, schmounded. Full speed ahead!"

To the ringing of the school bell, the three of us marched into our classroom, ready for action—and stopped dead when we saw who was sitting at our teacher's desk:

An absolute stranger.

Chapter Fourteen

Meeting Mr. Stenchy Pits

IS STARE WAS as black as the inside of a panther's nostril, his shaved head gleamed like the world's ugliest Christmas ornament, and his bulky body made the desk look like doll furniture.

Who the heck is that? I thought.

"Who the heck is that?" said Benny.

"Siddown!" growled the giant.

Stunned, we found our seats. And then I recognized him. It was Mr. Stenchy Pits, the man we'd bumped into outside the comics store. I remembered us saying that he was either a spy or a preschool teacher.

But that had been a joke. So what in the world was he doing in our classroom?

"My name," he said, glaring around the room, "is Mr.

Kardoz. I am your substitute." His voice had a foreign flavor to it.

Fifteen hands immediately shot into the air.

"You." He jerked his chin at Gabi Acosta. "Pigtail Girl. What is your question?"

"What happened to Mr. Chu?"

"I do not know and I do not care," Mr. Kardoz rumbled. "For today, he does not exist. I am your teacher."

Benny and I exchanged a horrified look. Was it already too late for Mr. Chu?

Turning around in her seat, Tina gave us a grim nod. She was right—grounding or no grounding, if we didn't act now, we would lose our favorite teacher for good.

And get stuck with someone who looked like he'd rather be strangling ferrets than teaching kids.

"Now," growled the substitute, "who is the most trust-worthy student?"

Tyler's hand shot into the air, followed closely by Amrita's and Cheyenne's. Mr. Kardoz raked his gaze over Tyler and read my classmate's soul. "You?" he said. "I think not. You have the look of a troublemaker. Maybe I give you detention, Midget Boy."

"But I haven't done anything!" Tyler protested.

Yet, I thought.

Big Pete raised his hand. "I think the politically correct term is *Height-Challenged Boy.*"

Glowering, the giant purred, "Maybe I give you both detention. Today, after school."

"But that's not fair!" Tyler whined.

"Fair?" Mr. Kardoz snapped. "Fair is cotton candy and pony rides. Life is not fair. *Two* days' detention." When Tyler wisely shut up, the substitute's attention shifted to Amrita, who looked sweeter than three bagfuls of Halloween candy. "You, Glasses Girl, what page of your math book is the class studying?"

"Page thirty-seven, Mr. Kardoz," she said.

"Open your books," the giant commanded.

When a bunch of us moaned in protest, Mr. Kardoz raised a furry eyebrow. "You forget," he crooned, "that I have absolute power here. If I say you will read your books standing on your head, then that is what you will do."

A nervous chuckle squirted out of one of my classmates.

"That's it!" roared the substitute. "Everyone up against the wall and onto your heads!"

We exchanged horrified and puzzled looks.

"Now!" yelled Mr. Kardoz.

With much dragging of feet, my class made its way over to the wall, math books in hand. The giant roared with laughter at our pitiful attempts to do a headstand. When he'd laughed enough, he ordered us back to our seats.

Could this man be one of the were-hyenas? He was certainly cruel enough.

As I sat down, a much-folded wad of paper landed on my desk. Unfurling it, I deciphered Benny's scrawl:

We gotta get out of here now! Time to save Mr. Chu!

Benny's eyes were dark with worry. I started to scribble a return note, then happened to glance up into Mr. Kardoz's suspicious scowl. Dropping my gaze to my math book, I waited. No sense in tempting him to make us run laps while juggling homework. When the substitute's attention wandered elsewhere, I held up a palm to Benny in a "wait" gesture and mouthed, *Recess.*

His lips clamped tight in frustration, but he nodded. And we got on with the unique brand of torture that only a sadistic sub can dish out.

At recess, Tina wouldn't leave us alone. Following Benny and me from the monkey bars, to the swings, to the field, she hounded us for more details about the whole were-hyena problem. At first we resisted, but after last night, I knew we'd need all the help we could get. Finally, I filled her in.

"So the way to cure Mr. Chu is to behead this 'alpha hyena'?" she said.

"Or hang the amulet around its neck," I said, kicking a stray soccer ball to Benny. Sometimes I think better when I'm moving a ball around.

"Okay, okay . . ." Tina fiddled with the beads on one of her braids, seeming to sort through everything we'd told her.

Benny kicked the ball back, hard and wide. "Enough talk. Time for action."

I retrieved it from the bushes. "I agree. But first let's figure out a plan."

"Here it is," said Benny. "First, we bust out of school. Then we make it up as we go along."

"But—" I began.

"Sounds like a plan to me," said Benny. He checked to

see if any of the yard-duty teachers were looking our way, and then said, "Come on, Carlos."

I shrugged at Tina. "When he's like this, it's easier to just go with it."

She folded her arms. "Let's see where that gets you."

Leading the way across the field, Benny pretended to wander aimlessly. But as I followed, we steadily made our way toward the gate in the chain-link fence. Our ticket to freedom.

Ten feet away, we made a final check. No teachers anywhere near; no kids either. Perfect. I could see Tina across the field, casually glancing in our direction. Did she know something that we didn't?

"Let's go!" whispered Benny.

We closed the distance in a rush, I put my hand to the gate, and a voice with a Texas twang said, "Going somewhere, boys?"

Busted.

We spun, trying to hide our guilty expressions.

"Us?" said Benny. "Just admiring the fence. Solid construction!"

"Uh-huh," said our principal, Mrs. Johnson. "You know, this ain't my first rodeo." Where in the world had she sprung from?

I raised my hands. "You got us. But we're on a life-and-death mission for Mr. Chu." I tried to stick close to the truth while still being vague.

Her eyes narrowed. "Mr. Chu is at home."

"We know," I said, "and our mission will help get him back in school."

Her mouth pursed. "You know, you can put your boots in the oven, but that won't make 'em biscuits."

"Excuse me?" Benny said.

"Calling something by a label doesn't make it so." Mrs. Johnson aimed one of her long fingers at Benny and me. "I know what you're really trying to do, and it won't work."

"You do?" I said. Did she really know all about the were-hyena?

"Of course," said the principal. "I didn't just fall off the turnip truck. I know when kids are trying to ditch school."

"Ohhh," I said, glancing at Benny. He pushed his palms downward in a "chill out" gesture. He had a point. Real heroes don't get their principal to solve their problems. "Um, you caught us fair and square."

"Let that be a lesson to you," said Mrs. Johnson. "Now go play."

"Yes, ma'am," we said.

As we trudged past her onto the field, Benny said, "If you don't mind my asking, how did you know we were making a break for it?"

One corner of Mrs. Johnson's mouth twitched. She tapped her temple. "Principal ESP."

I didn't doubt it for a second.

When Tina caught up with Benny and me on the far

side of the field, she didn't have to say "I told you so." But she did anyway.

"It's too tricky to escape during school hours," she said. "Even if you get past that fence, someone will turn you in."

Benny's fists went to his hips. He gave her a look as full of attitude as a second-rate rapper in a third-rate music video. "Oh, and I suppose you've got a better idea, Miss Nosy?"

A smile spread, slow as syrup, across her face. "As a matter of fact, I do."

"Are you gonna tell us?" I asked. "Or make us guess?"

"How do kids get out of school without anyone causing a fuss?" she asked.

I lifted a shoulder. "Doctor's note?"

"Field trip."

Benny frowned. "Huh?"

"Our class," she said. "Field trip. Museum. Get it?"

Clapping one hand to his head and the other to his chest, Benny slumped dramatically, like the idea was so bad it hurt. "Genius!" he said. "Only one tiny problem: the field trip has to happen *today*, and we don't even have permission slips."

Her smile was smugger than a roomful of know-it-alls. "But Mr. Car-Nose doesn't know that."

"That's *Kardoz*." I could feel a smile tugging at my own lips. "You know, you're pretty sneaky. For a girl."

"Thanks," said Tina. "I'm sure you have some redeeming qualities, too."

Chapter Fifteen

Grand Theft Amulet

NEVER UNDERESTIMATE the appeal of a break in humdrum school-day routine—for kids and teachers both. A bit of fast-talking, a convincing lie or two, and—*boom*—there we were at the museum. When we walked through the doors, Ms. Icaza was waiting with a broad smile. "Welcome, children! We're so pleased you came to learn about African culture."

Mr. Kardoz glowered. "Children," he muttered. "Culture. In my day, the two never met."

Because no docents were on duty this early, Ms. Icaza decided to show us around the new exhibit herself. We all trooped upstairs. Our giant sub brought up the rear.

After passing through a bunch of Greek statues of

naked people (and listening to Tyler's dumb comments about them), we rounded the corner into the new exhibit. Big Pete gasped.

Standing directly in front of him was a tall wooden sculpture of a horned man with sinister, hooded eyes. I would've gasped myself if I'd been in front. But that was no reason to skip teasing Pete.

"What's wrong?" said José. "Too much like looking in the mirror?"

"Oooh, sssspooky!" Benny joked. Even though I could tell the exhibit creeped him out, too.

Big Pete scowled and raised a fist. But after our sub gave him the eye, he refrained from pounding anybody.

An eerie flute trilled in the background as we entered the exhibit. Everything smelled seriously old and musty, like the back of your grandpa's closet, only worse. I could tell this exhibit still wasn't quite finished. Not all of the items were in display cases, and most were missing those informational cards.

Ms. Icaza went into her talk about the mystical ceremonies of the Yoruba and the Dan. "These were a people who loved ritual," she said. "They had ceremonies for baby naming, for deaths, for weddings—"

"For bathroom breaks?" AJ asked. Kids chuckled.

The museum lady made a facc. "First floor, beside the entrance," she said. "Now, everyone, come have a look at these staffs set with gems. They're priceless." The class pressed forward, but Benny and I hung back. To one side, the amulets hung in a dark little corner.

Behind us, Mr. Kardoz leaned against a wall, scowling as he texted someone on his phone. Probably asking the Kremlin for his next assassination target.

"So what's our move?" Benny muttered, bringing his head close to mine.

"Knock down a statue?" I suggested.

He grimaced. "Over too quick. Um, I could pick a fight with Tyler?"

I glanced at Mr. Kardoz. "He'd give you detention, and then we'd never get free. Umm . . ."

Tina stuck her head in between ours, making me jump. "It's obvious," she said.

"Oh yeah?" said Benny. "What?"

"Two of us fake fight, to distract everybody. The other one grabs the necklace."

I blinked. It was actually a pretty good plan.

"Okay," I said, "let's do it. I'll make the snatch."

Benny cocked his head, not wanting to seem too keen on her idea. "It's not a totally terrible plan. I guess it might work."

Just then, beyond a knot of our classmates, I noticed Ms. Icaza watching us. "Chill," I murmured, drifting away from them. The museum worker flashed me a smile and I returned it, making an I'm-impressed-with-your-place face.

She gestured at a seriously whacked-out mask with tusks and spikes and two sets of eyes. "The Dan designed this *bu gle* mask to frighten the bejeezus out of people, and as you can see, it still works." Several girls tittered. When Ms. Icaza began explaining the uses of the mask to my classmates, I ambled over to where the amulets hung. A velvet rope and some low posts were all that protected them from visitors' grubby hands.

I chewed the inside of my cheek. Now that I was here, I had some doubts. How would I grab the necklace and hide it on me while standing in plain view of twenty-seven kids and two adults?

I scanned the space. The museum might even have security cameras.

The things we think of too late.

Across the room, Benny and Tina had already started up their act. No time for second thoughts. I had to roll with it.

Benny appeared to be teaching Tina some kind of judo hold. Shaking her head, she tried to show him how it was really done. They tussled, back and forth, drawing closer and closer to a statue of a tall dude with a pointy head.

A few kids noticed them, but so far both adults were unaware.

I wiped my sweaty palms on my jeans. Any second now . . .

Grabbing Benny by the shoulders, Tina spun him around in a complicated move. But she used a bit too much body

English. Benny stumbled and bumped the statue, which swayed alarmingly.

ANNNKH-ANNNKH-ANNNKH! honked the fire alarm.

¡Santa María! I jumped like a grasshopper on a griddle. Glancing around, I caught Big Pete slinking away from the alarm with a guilty smirk.

For a second, I was tempted to rat him out. Then I remembered my mission. When a plan goes wrong, heroes improvise.

My classmates milled about, confused. The adults were distracted.

Showtime.

Drawing on acting skills I'd barely tapped in the class play, I pretended to shrink against the wall in fear. Through the velvet rope, I staggered backward. A glance confirmed my target. Hitting the wall, I groped behind me for the hyena amulet.

There! I snatched the necklace off its hook with a jerk and stuffed it down the back of my pants. Okay, it was a little weird to have a mystical amulet in my tighty-whities, but in the heat of the moment, that was the only safe place I could think of.

Pushing off the wall, I joined the swirling group of kids. Mr. Kardoz and Ms. Icaza both bellowed instructions that nobody could hear over the alarm. José snatched a tall staff from the display and raised it in the en garde position, ready to defend himself in case something came to life.

With a look of horror, Ms. Icaza rushed across and took the artifact away from him. Someone else knocked over a statue, and the museum worker hurried to right it.

Unable to make himself heard, Mr. Kardoz got physical. He spread his arms wide and steered students toward the exit stairs like a demented snowplow, mouthing, *Go, go, go!*

I caught Benny's eye and nodded. Mission accomplished. Just as we hurried into the stairwell, something made me glance back. Past the giant substitute teacher, I saw the trim figure, gleaming hair, and penetrating eyes of the museum director, Mr. Sharkawy.

And he was staring straight at Benny and me.

Chapter Sixteen

Mr. Chu's Terrible, Horrible, No Good, Very Bad Day

BY THE TIME we marched out the doors and down the museum steps, the fire trucks had arrived. A squad of yellow-clad firefighters rushed past us and into the museum. They ignored Mr. Sharkawy's protests that it was a false alarm, and told us they'd have to check each floor before letting everyone back inside.

His face a thundercloud, the museum director stalked over to where Benny and I were standing. "You! You're responsible for this."

We raised our hands in surrender. "Not us," Benny said.

Snug between my tighty-whities and my skin, the hyena amulet radiated warmth, almost like a living thing. I shuddered. I forced myself not to reach back and pluck it out of my shorts.

Mr. Sharkawy leaned down and got into our faces, wagging his finger like a club. "I don't know why you did it, and I don't know how, but you little troublemakers bloody well did it."

"We didn't do anything," I said. "Honest."

"Confess!" cried the museum director.

Sweat rolled down my forehead, despite the cool morning. I knew if I gave up the real culprit, Big Pete would pound me into the ground so hard I'd pop out in Antarctica. Nobody squeals on a bully and lives.

"What is this?" a deep voice growled. For the first time, Mr. Kardoz's massive bulk was as welcome as a snow cone in the Sahara.

"Your students pulled my fire alarm," said the museum director, sidling back from him like a hyena from a hungry lion. "I'm absolutely certain of it."

"Did you catch them in the act?" asked the substitute.

"No," said Mr. Sharkawy. "They—"

"Do you have any proof that they did it?"

"No, but—"

"Bah, enough!" The giant shouldered Mr. Sharkawy

aside, grabbing me by the arm and steering us away. "You are bothering my students," he rumbled. "Nobody bothers my students but me."

I could've kissed our sub. If he hadn't been a huge, scary guy who strangled weasels for fun, that is.

He led us off to join the others. Somehow, Benny and I resisted the temptation to stick out our tongues at the fuming Mr. Sharkawy.

As everyone lined up on the sidewalk for the trip back to school, Tina kept her distance, giving us the "be cool" signal. Benny and I watched Ms. Icaza talking with a firefighter and the museum director snarling into his cell phone like a mad dog.

When I saw Mr. Sharkawy foaming at the mouth, a thought struck me. I nudged Benny. "You think *he* could be the one who bit Mr. Chu?" I said. "The alpha hyena?"

Almost as if he'd heard us, the museum director turned our way and bared his teeth.

"If he's not," Benny said, "at the very least, he's an alpha weirdo."

"Too true," I said. "Hey, by the way, nice job tussling with Tina."

He tried to look modest. "Thanks."

"Looked like you were really enjoying it," I said.

"Well, it was . . ."

I grinned and broke into song. "Benny and Tina, sitting

in a tree, K-I-S-S-I-N-G. First comes love, then comes marriage—"

And then Benny showed me what tussling was *really* all about.

As our class started walking back to school, Benny and I tried to take advantage of our freedom and slip away from the group. But Mr. Kardoz's KGB training must have included seeing out of the back of his head. He caught us before we'd gone twenty feet.

Back in school, at the tail end of lunch period, Benny and I regrouped.

"Well, here we are," I said.

"Yup," said Benny.

"Right back where we started."

"Uh-huh." Benny made a face. "Stuck on the inside, and trying to get out."

I nodded. "I think this is what Mr. Chu would call ironic."

Now that we had the amulet, Benny was all in favor of either: (a) busting out of school right away; or (b) trying out the amulet on every suspicious-looking person, starting with our substitute teacher and ending with Mr. Sharkawy.

I convinced him that: (c) since it was lunchtime, we really should eat something first; (d) there were more suspicious people in Monterrosa than we had time to visit in a week;

and (e) if we hung the necklace around Mr. Sharkawy's neck, he'd know that we stole it, and he'd call Benny's dad to arrest us.

Since Benny really hates being arrested by his dad, he agreed to at least have lunch with me. (Good thing, too. Lunch on Taco Thursday is one of the cafeteria's most realistically foodlike meals.)

After we dumped our leftovers in the trash and our trays and plates on the dirty stack, Benny and I found a quiet corner of the playground. Our goal? To sort out our next move.

"You know what worries me?" I said.

"That they're putting fewer M&M's in every bag?" said Benny.

I leaned on the chain-link fence. "Besides that. What worries me is how we're going to get out of the house after we're home, since we're supposed to be grounded."

He lifted a shoulder. "Out the window, like always. What's the big deal?"

"Um, maybe you're not familiar with the word *grounded*," I said. "They'll be watching us like hawks."

Benny's forehead crinkled. "Oh, yeah."

"And we've got another problem," I said.

"Oh, yeah?"

"Since there's more than one were-hyena, we need to figure out how to tell which one is the alpha. We won't get a second chance with the amulet."

Benny was lost in thought for a moment. "Mr. Chu knows," he said in a small voice.

My throat went dry. The only person who could identify the alpha was going to turn hyena-man himself in a few hours, as soon as the moon rose. I took a deep breath. "Then maybe we should . . . go visit him?"

Benny gulped. "Let's do it now, before school's out. The longer we wait, the more hyena-fied he'll be."

I couldn't argue with that logic. We hunted down Tina on the tetherball court and somehow convinced her to distract Mrs. Johnson. (In this case, "somehow" meant promising Tina that she could come along when we faced the alpha hyena.)

Tina must have held up her end of the bargain, because this time Benny and I managed to sneak out the side gate without detection.

I wagged my head. "And to think we spent all that time and effort on the field-trip plan."

Benny snorted a laugh. "We should've just unleashed Tina on Mrs. Johnson in the first place."

"At least we got the amulet out of it."

Still, it didn't pay to get too cocky. We crept along a line of eucalyptus trees until we were well out of sight of Monterrosa Elementary, then stood up and walked like normal people.

It felt weird being the only ones out of school. We saw no other kids—except for some rug rats with their moms.

A few grown-ups stared at us curiously. But Benny kept marching along the sidewalk like we belonged there, and no one bothered to stop us.

Even so, I was relieved when we turned off the busier streets and into Mr. Chu's neighborhood. Here, fewer people were out and about. The houses looked older, the yards shaggier. A scruffy yellow mutt barked like he meant to rip us to shreds and didn't shut up until we'd gone way down the street. Those sharp white teeth gave me the jitters. All I could think about was were-hyenas on the loose.

Finally we reached Mr. Chu's house. From the curb, it looked normal enough. Cocoa-brown shingle roof, the usual number of doors and windows. The yard bloomed with drought-resistant plants like deer grass, lupine, and sage. (And yes, I got an A on my drought-resistant gardening report.)

As we started up the walkway, hummingbirds fluttered in my stomach. I caught Benny's arm.

"Wait. We should have a weapon."

"What?" he said.

"In case Mr. Chu gets out of control."

Benny flapped a hand. "Don't be ridiculous. He won't hurt us—we're his favorite students."

"So is Tina," I said, "and he fought her over a chicken."

But Benny wasn't listening. "He's not evil, just sick." He snapped his fingers. "Hey, we should bring him something."

"It's a little late to pick up candy," I said.

Glancing around, his eye fell on the clumps of purple lupine. Benny ripped up a handful. "This'll do."

"Sure," I said. "If he's so far gone that he can't tell you raided his garden." I scanned the yard for a weapon, but nothing presented itself.

Benny strolled boldly up to the front door and rapped on it. Nothing. I pushed the doorbell and we waited. More nothing.

His forehead creased in a frown. "You don't suppose he's already . . ." He made monster claws.

"Not yet," I said. "It's still daylight. Maybe he's napping? We should go."

"I bet he's in back," said Benny, hopping off the doorstep and heading around the house.

"Wait!" I said. "We can't just—"

But apparently we could. Benny marched over to the tall wooden fence, worked the gate latch, and stepped into Mr. Chu's backyard.

My pulse raced. My hands went clammy.

Afraid? Oh, just a little. We were entering an actual teacher's backyard! Without permission! Few kids could claim to have done that. Checking the street behind us for witnesses, I followed Benny.

The side yard was sunk in shadows. Laurels, a sycamore, and some massive bushes I didn't know the names of overhung a khaki-colored strip of lawn. An odd grunting came from somewhere ahead of us.

"Mr. Chu?" I called, grabbing a broom that was leaning against the house. It wasn't a real weapon, but it was something.

"It's Benny and Carlos," said Benny. "From class?"

No reply.

"Do you think something happened to him?" Benny asked.

I shrugged. My bare arms tingled like they were being brushed by termite wings.

Benny bit his lip.

We crept forward along the flagstone path that stretched beside the house.

"Mr. Chu?" I called again. "We just wanted to see how you were—"

Stepping around the corner, we both stopped dead. My chin dropped so far, it practically hit my chest.

Wearing only a blue T-shirt and some Hello Kitty boxer shorts, Monterrosa Elementary's Teacher of the Year was vigorously rubbing his butt on the ground, muttering, "Mine! Mine!"

"On the bright side," said Benny. "At least he's wearing undies."

Chapter Seventeen

Teacher Creature

WARILY, we approached Mr. Chu, stopping a good ten feet away. He glanced up at us, giggled, and scuttled over to the nearest laurel trunk. Once more, he did the butt-rubbing.

I winced. Some things you really don't want to see your teacher doing.

"Um, how's it going, Mr. Chu?" said Benny.

"Stellar!" said our were-teacher. "Simply stellar!" His grin was wide enough to drive a truck through, his new hair was matted, and his eyes looked puffy and feverish. Let's just say he wasn't ready for class picture day.

I gripped my broom. Benny edged forward and cautiously laid the lupine on the ground before him.

"We, uh, brought you some flowers," I said.

He chuckled, long and loony. "Loveliness!" Then he leaned over and took a huge bite of the purple flowers. After several vigorous chews, he spat out the petals. "Bad flower!"

Benny cleared his throat. "Carlos and I wanted to see how you were feeling."

Twice our teacher raked the ground with his foot, just like Zeppo does when he's marking his territory. Then Mr. Chu's eyes cleared and he frowned up at us. "What are you doing with my broom? And why aren't you two in school?" For a second, he seemed almost like his old self.

I tossed the broom aside. "We were worried, uh, that you . . ." I began.

Then the moment passed, and he scrambled across the yard after a bird. We trailed behind him.

"Mr. Chu!" said Benny. "We need to ask you something important."

"Cat poop!" Our teacher turned his back on us, sticking his face down into the tall grasses.

"No, we really do," I said.

He shook his head and indicated the grass. "Cat poop. Disguises your scent!" Our teacher cackled, flopped down on his back, and started rolling where the cat had done its business.

"Eeeww!" cried Benny and I together.

We rushed to his side, each taking a hand, and tried to drag him off. Mr. Chu only wriggled harder, like Zeppo does when he finds a dead seal on the beach. And as it turned out, our teacher was about as easy to move as a dead seal. When at last Mr. Chu had gotten enough stink on him, he sat up.

"We need to ask about the, um, thing that bit you," I said, fanning the air.

Our teacher's eyes grew as big as tortillas. "Straaannnge doggie."

"That's right," said Benny, crouching beside him. "What did it look like?"

"The doggie?" he asked.

I squatted down. "Yes. What did the doggie look like?" At last we were getting somewhere.

Mr. Chu studied a cloud and seemed to consider the question. "Like doggie," he said.

I shook my head. Benny clapped his hand to his forehead. The eye-watering stench of cat poop wafted around us.

"Mr. Chu," I said, "remember how you're always telling us to add details to our writing?"

Idly, he scratched his side. His nostrils flared, drawing his attention away to the world of scents.

"Just give us some details about the dog that bit you," said Benny. "Please?"

Head lolling around on his neck, Mr. Chu scowled. At last his eyes focused. "Fangs, sharp fangs," he said. "Black . . . eyes. Crazy eyes."

The memory seemed to be disturbing him. His lips

curled into a sneer, and it seemed like his canine teeth had grown longer and yellower. Suddenly Mr. Chu's hands clawed the air. "*Bad* doggie . . ."

Benny and I stood, taking a step back. I wished I hadn't tossed the broom.

"Uh, yeah," I said. "We want to stop the bad doggie. Anything that might help us recognize it? Fur color? Height?"

"Special markings?" asked Benny.

One of Mr. Chu's hands swatted at the left side of his chest. "White"—he struggled for the word—"blaze. Here."

As if the words had used up all his humanness, our were-teacher snarled and dropped to all fours. His eyes rolled back into his head until all we could see were the whites. An eerie keening, like "Eee-hee-hee-heeee" poured from our teacher's throat.

¡Dios mío!

"Uh," I croaked.

Goose bumps rippled in a wave over my neck, shoulders, and arms. With feet as clumsy as concrete blocks, I backed up the way we'd come.

"F-feel b-better soon," Benny stammered, joining me. As we sidled away, neither of us could tear our gaze from the sight of our teacher's freak-out. When we were maybe five feet from the corner of the house, Mr. Chu flung up one hand to the sky.

"Moooon!" he yowled, his eyes as white and blank as two Ping-Pong balls.

That did it. Benny and I yelped, spun, and broke into a shambling run.

"Coming soooon!" Mr. Chu's howled prediction chased us around the corner of the house, into the front yard, and down the street.

My heart was thudding so fast, it must've sounded like a tap-dance class for octopuses. Gasping and gibbering, Benny and I ran for blocks, not stopping until we reached Porter Street. There we stood panting, hands on knees, until we caught our breath.

"That . . . was something," I said.

"Yeah," said Benny.

"He's gotten much more . . . hyena-fied."

"Much," he agreed.

My eyes met his. "You know what this means, don't you?"

Benny nodded. "If we don't succeed tonight, we'll be holding classes in the zoo."

I straightened up. "Then let's get cracking."

On the walk back, Benny took an unexpected right at the corner of Grove Street.

"School's this way," I said, pointing left.

"No duh," he said.

I crossed my arms. "Don't play around. We'll be in enough trouble as it is."

Benny got that light in his eyes. "I've been thinking. . . ."

"Never a good sign," I said.

"And I think you're right."

I pretended to feel his forehead. "Now I *know* you're woozy."

"You said our parents would probably keep us locked in after school."

"Probably?" I said. "We'll be grounded for a week."

Drifting up the sidewalk toward Main Street, Benny kept talking. He knew I'd follow. "So sneaking out to catch Mr. Chu's maker tonight will be hard enough without adding another sneak-out before that."

"Hang on. Why would we need to sneak out before that?"

"To check with Mrs. Tamasese, of course—to learn more about the alpha hyena and his powers. We've got to be ready."

What we'd just seen at Mr. Chu's house must have shaken me more than I knew. Otherwise, how to explain what happened next? I planted my feet, stopped dead on the sidewalk, and did something I'd almost never done before.

I told Benny, "No."

"No?"

Emotions fizzed inside me like soda in a shaken-up can. "No! No more breaking rules and getting in trouble."

Benny offered a half smile. "But that's what we do."

"Not anymore." My hands slashed the air. "It hasn't gotten us anything but detention and being grounded."

"What do you mean?"

"It hasn't cured Mr. Chu." My eyes prickled and my jaw tightened. "I'm going to do something we should have done a long time ago."

"Change our socks?" Benny was trying to keep things light, but I wasn't joking around. Not this time.

"I'm going to the cops with this," I said.

Benny's eyes got huge, and his hands came up. "Whoa, whoa, whoa! Bad idea. The last thing we need is to get the cops involved."

In the face of his sureness, I wobbled for a moment. But the sight of Mr. Chu's rolled-back eyeballs had decided me.

"We're in way over our heads," I said. "Come with me."

"Are you crazy?"

I reached out to him. "Let's go to your dad and tell him everything. He's got to believe us."

"Why would he? *Your* dad didn't believe us."

I drew myself up. "We've got to at least *try*. We're not professional monster hunters, Benny. We're just kids."

His cheeks reddened and his eyes held a hurt look. "*You* may chicken out," he said in a tight voice, "but I'm not missing my chance to be a hero."

"Don't be stupid," I said, and instantly regretted it.

Benny's face froze. "*You're* the stupid one." Turning on

his heel, he fled down the sidewalk in the direction of the comics store.

"Benny!" I cried, taking a couple of strides after him. But my steps faltered. I'd known as soon as I said it that the police station was the right place to go. And with Benny or without him, that's exactly where I was headed.

Chapter Eighteen

Shocks and Bonds

THE NEXT FEW blocks were a blur. My mind churned like chilies in a grinder. Endlessly, it turned over my argument with Benny, Mr. Chu's worsening condition, and the teensy little problem of what the heck I was going to tell the police to convince them to act.

I couldn't believe Benny had gone off on his own like that. From the first time we'd met in kindergarten, we'd been practically inseparable. I couldn't believe I'd told him no. I tried to think of things from his side. He probably just didn't want to look like he was running to his daddy.

Maybe he had a point. . . .

This is the downside of being the kind of kid who always overthinks things.

I was so distracted that the toot of a car horn made me jump.

A bronze Toyota pulled to the curb ahead of me, and the passenger-side window slid down. A familiar PTA-mom-looking face with salt-and-pepper hair peered out.

"Is that Carlos?" asked the museum lady.

"Oh, hi, Ms. Icaza," I said.

Her smile was as warm as fresh-baked sugar cookies. "You look like a man on a mission," she said. "Need a ride?"

Now, I'm not a complete idiot. I know kids aren't supposed to take rides from strangers. But since I'd met her twice, Ms. Icaza wasn't technically a stranger. Plus, my mom had been in L.A. for a couple days, and I was really missing her. Right then I needed a sympathetic, momlike ear.

"Um, maybe . . ." I said, wavering. "I'm going to the police station?"

The museum worker turned off her car, got out, and joined me on the sidewalk. "The police?" she said. "Are you going to surrender yourself to the truant officer?"

"Not exactly," I said. "It kind of has to do with . . . shapeshifting."

She didn't scoff, she didn't laugh. Instead, Ms. Icaza's eyes went round with interest. "Really?" she said. "Tell me."

I took a deep breath and decided to use her as a dry run for the story I'd give the police. "It's my teacher," I said. "He's turning into a were-hyena."

Then I proceeded to hit the low points of the past

couple days, leaving out the bit where Big Pete pulled the fire alarm and Benny and I borrowed her museum's amulet.

Sometime during the tale, we climbed into her car and she drove slowly away. Most grown-ups barely listen to kids; they only wait for their turn to tell you what's what. But Ms. Icaza was not most grown-ups. When I finished, she stayed silent.

"I—I know it sounds crazy," I said at last, "but—"

She held up a palm. "No. No, it doesn't sound crazy. Unlikely, yes. Bizarre, yes. But I believe you."

"You do?"

Her hand patted mine. "I do. 'There are more things in heaven and earth, Horatio, than are dreamt of in your philosophy.'"

"Huh?"

Ms. Icaza smiled. "Shakespeare. It means there are still unknowns, still miracles on this planet. Science doesn't know everything. In fact, Mr. Sharkawy and I saw some strange sights when we were in Africa, so I don't find the whole idea of shapeshifters so hard to believe."

"That's great," I said. My heart suddenly felt lighter. "Will you come with me to see the cops? They might take me more seriously if I've got a grown-up along."

Turning a corner, Ms. Icaza said, "I'll do even better than that."

"You will?"

"Absolutely. I'll help you cure your teacher."

"That'd be terrific!" I said. Then I noticed which direction we were heading. "Um, but the police station is behind us."

Ms. Icaza gave me a conspiratorial look. "First, we're going to the museum."

"The museum?" This didn't seem like the best time to take in some culture.

"Not everything we brought back is part of the Africa exhibit," she said. "Mr. Sharkawy collected other occult objects and ancient texts, and I think we may have something to help cure shapeshifters."

A worm of guilt writhed in my belly. How could I tell her not to bother going back for the amulet because it was already in my pocket?

"Oh, really?" I asked. "What kinds of things?"

"Rare translations of ancient rituals, as well as herbs from tribal shamans."

I relaxed again. "Okay by me. That sounds good."

In under five minutes Ms. Icaza had parked her car in the museum lot and was leading me toward the employees' entrance. A sudden thought jolted me, and I balked.

"What's wrong?" she asked.

"Mr. Sharkawy," I said. "He won't help us. He hates me and Benny."

She flapped her hand, dismissing my worry. "That's ridiculous. He doesn't hate you two."

"He doesn't?"

Ms. Icaza's laugh chimed like mission bells. "He hates *all* children. But never fear, he loves the supernatural even more than he loathes kids."

"If you say so . . ." I said, letting her usher me into the building. Being anywhere near the guy made me nervous, but maybe Ms. Icaza could keep him in line.

Instead of taking me upstairs to the director's office, however, Ms. Icaza led the way down some steps to the basement level. The ceiling hung low, the walls were pea-soup green, and a permanent chill filled the air.

"Um, what about your boss?" I asked.

"Time is of the essence." She hurried along a corridor, fishing in her purse for a key ring. "I need you to start looking through the papers while I break the news to Mr. Sharkawy in a way that gets him on our side. It'll go faster if you're not there."

I liked the way she said "our side." Not to diss Mrs. Tamasese's advice, but it was a relief to have a grown-up more actively helping us with Mr. Chu's problem.

When Ms. Icaza opened up the storage room, the fluo-rescents flickered on overhead, bathing everything in a sickly greenish light. Stacks of shallow boxes about the size of paintings were leaning on one wall. Against another, a long table held rolls of brightly colored fabric and a row of what I guessed were African sculptures. They ranged from bearded weirdos and animal-headed dudes to earth-mother figures. Shelves filled the back half of this wide room, groaning under the weight of countless papers and scrolls.

"Wow." I sized up the racks. "Do I have to look through all of this?"

Ms. Icaza chuckled. "Not quite. The papers we brought back from Africa are right here." She indicated the two lowest shelves and passed me a box of disposable gloves. "Put these on to protect the documents."

As she turned to go, I said, "Wait. What am I looking for?"

"Descriptions of Yoruba and Bakongo shamanic rituals. I know I saw several dealing with animal possession."

My face must have reflected my doubts, because Ms. Icaza offered me a motherly smile. "Don't worry," she said, patting my shoulder, "we'll take care of you." Then she bustled out the door and closed it behind her with a click.

The harsh overhead light cast dramatic shadows on the sculptures. Too dramatic. The eyes of the biggest animal-headed dude were like pools of darkness, drawing me in. Could a carving hypnotize a person? Or could it come to life, like that evil doll Chucky?

I shuddered.

Then I took a deep breath and got a grip. We had important work to do and here I was, wasting time scaring myself. Slipping on a pair of ultrathin latex gloves, I got to work.

Time seemed to zip by as I paged through the crinkly old documents at a low worktable. I found plenty of references to rituals, but nothing about animal possession. The papers piled up. When at last I stood to stretch a kink out of my back, it suddenly struck me:

Where was Ms. Icaza?

She'd sounded like she meant to come right back. But it felt like at least a half hour had passed, maybe more. Had she gotten into trouble with her boss?

I shivered as an awful thought occurred. If Mr. Sharkawy was the alpha hyena, he wouldn't want us trying to cure Mr. Chu. In fact, he might do something drastic to his own employee to stop us.

Uh-oh.

I peeled off the gloves and tossed them onto the table. In a half-dozen strides, I stood at the door. I tried the knob.

Locked.

Hammering on the thick wood, I cried, "Hello? Ms. Icaza? Mr. Sharkawy? Anyone there?"

No answer. I pounded again.

And then I heard something that froze my bones to the marrow: a low, sinister chuckle.

"H-hello?" I called, voice wavering. "Who's there?"

Still no reply.

"The door's locked," I said. "I can't get out."

"Of course not," said an oily voice. "You're right where we want you."

"Mr. Sharkawy?" I said. "It's Carlos Rivera. Open up."

The chuckle lasted even longer this time, sounding positively unhinged.

"I'll do nothing of the sort," said the museum director when he'd finished his spooky laughing exercises. "The animal ancestors require a sacrifice, and guess what? You're it."

Híjole. I sagged in disbelief. My forehead rested against the door.

All I could think was, I really, really wished I'd listened to Benny.

Chapter Nineteen

Escapes of Wrath

MY SHOCK only lasted for a few heartbeats. Then the full awareness of my predicament sank in. Stark terror boiled along my veins, scorching its way through my body like molten lava.

"No!" I yelled, pounding my fists against the door. "You can't do this! I'm only in fourth grade!"

"The ancestors demand a sacrifice every moon. It's an honor to be chosen," said Mr. Sharkawy. His voice sounded so creepy, it felt like tarantulas were scuttling down my spine.

"I don't deserve the honor!" I cried. "I cheated on a pop quiz!"

"The ancients like fresh young offerings."

"But I'm *not* fresh." I pounded harder. "I forgot to change my underwear, and I haven't showered all week!"

"The gods have chosen," said Mr. Sharkawy.

I didn't like the sound of that at all. "Where's Ms. Icaza?"

"Someplace where she won't interfere," said the psycho museum director. "Prepare yourself. I'll return presently."

Poor Ms. Icaza. She was locked up, knocked out, or worse.

Poor me. She wouldn't be coming to save me.

At that point, I did what any self-respecting kid in my situation would've done. I screamed, I pleaded, and I threatened. None of it did any good. Mr. Sharkawy was either getting his jollies by listening to me freak out, or he'd gone off to do other creepy-museum-guy things. I couldn't tell.

Right then, I made a vow: no more telling grown-ups about our supernatural troubles. Not only was it bad form for a hero, but it had landed me in this predicament.

After rattling and kicking the door, I began exploring the room, searching for an escape route. Aside from the entrance, there was no way out. The storeroom was almost window-free, except for a single narrow, rectangular opening high on the far wall.

I dragged over a chair and climbed onto it. Teetering on tiptoe, I could *almost* reach the bottom of the window frame. Shoot. I added a pile of thick books and tried again. This time, my hand closed on the latch.

But no matter how much I tugged and twisted, it

wouldn't budge. I took a closer look. The lock had been sloppily painted over the last time this room was redone, probably back around the time of King Tut.

On a shelf of tools, I found a small hammer that looked like something you'd use to knock dirt off of fossils. I whacked the latch with it.

The stupid thing still wouldn't budge.

How long had Mr. Sharkawy been gone? I wondered. The room had no clock. I patted my pockets, remembering at last to look for my cell phone. Not only could I learn the time, I could call for help!

And then I recalled: my phone was right where I left it. In my desk. At school.

Right then, I'm not ashamed to say I threw a small tantrum. Nothing like the ones my drama-queen little sister can manage, but it involved plenty of yelling and whining and battering my fists on the table.

"Not fair!" I cried.

When I stopped abusing the table, I realized maybe I could use it. After dumping everything onto the floor, I hauled the heavy thing underneath the window. Then I set the chair on top.

Climbing onto it, I once again whacked the window latch. Still stuck. That thing was frozen harder than a truant officer's heart.

"Gnnnagh!" I made one last swing with all my might.

And hit the glass. *Kssshh!* went the windowpane.

A realization dawned. Duh. If the window won't open, break it.

In less than a minute, I'd knocked out most of the glass. At last! But then, looking it over carefully, I realized two things: (a) even if I could avoid slicing myself to ribbons on the stubborn teeth of glass still in the frame, I was (b) too big to fit through that narrow gap.

Dang it.

A fresh breeze blew from outside, taunting me with the tang of eucalyptus.

Although nothing showed through the window but a gently sloping bank of ice plant, I heard the groan and rattle of a truck nearby.

"Hey!" I screamed. "Help! I'm locked in!"

Beep-beep-beep went the truck as it backed up.

"Help! Someone help me!"

Metal bins boomed and thumped as the trash truck emptied them.

Over and over I screamed, until my throat was as raw as an all-sushi buffet. The truck drove off. Nobody came.

It was starting to look like the animal ancestors might enjoy some piping-hot Carlos Rivera after all. And that thought sent a new wave of fear crashing through me.

I scurried around the room collecting the bright African fabric, a sheaf of colored paper, small sculptures—anything I could throw through the window to attract attention. With a Magic Marker, I scrawled HELP, I'M BEING HELD CAPTIVE!—CARLOS on a bunch of the sheets.

Out it all went. Most of the junk landed within a foot or two of the building, but I managed to use a hand-carved staff to shove some of the fabric and papers a little farther up the slope.

I hoped it was far enough.

Climbing down from the table, I lost my balance and toppled. Just in time, my hands braced on the cement floor, breaking my fall.

I found myself face-to-face with a steel floor grate. From the look of things, this basement storeroom had originally been designed so people could hose it down to clean it. (Although nobody had cleaned out this place in a *long* time.)

The grate measured maybe one foot on each side—big enough to accommodate a fair volume of water.

Or a desperate fourth-grade boy.

Sticking my fingers through the holes in the grid, I pulled upward. The heavy grate barely stirred. Jeez, was everything in this place stuck?

Voices echoed from the corridor. Mr. Sharkawy and his assistants, coming to take me away.

My pulse raced. It was now or never.

Squatting over the grate and planting my feet, I heaved for all I was worth. This time the steel square came up in my hands. A strong whiff of mold and sewage followed it.

I turned my face away and tried to breathe through my mouth.

A key rattled in the door lock.

No time for squeamishness. I dropped the grate with a clang and stuffed my legs into the hole. As my prison door swung open, I levered myself forward, dropped into the chute—

And got stuck under my armpits.

Mr. Sharkawy strode into the room, followed by a ridiculously tall man and a snaky-looking woman. All three gaped. They stopped dead at the sight of me, stuck like a mole in a hole.

I gave a nervous chuckle. "Fancy meeting you here."

"Grab him!" the museum director yelled.

Mr. Stretch and Snake Woman charged forward.

In a last, reckless move, I raised my arms above my head and rolled my shoulders forward, like an Olympic diver. It worked.

Foof! I slipped down the shaft. Mr. Stretch's hand just grazed my fingertips as I disappeared.

"Nooo!" wailed Mr. Sharkawy.

The tube reminded me of the chute at a water park, minus the water and the fun. But unlike the thrill ride, my trip was over in mere seconds.

Whump-splash! I crashed onto a hard floor ten feet below. Something made a crumbly sound. After making sure it wasn't my leg bones, I stood up in ankle-high water.

The sewer stench was foul enough to make my nose want to crawl back into my head. Light filtering down from the storeroom revealed a section of dark brick tunnel. Something made that cracking-crumbling sound again.

"Don't worry!" The light dimmed as Mr. Sharkawy's face filled the opening above. "I'll save you."

"Yeah, and then you'll sacrifice me," I said.

He wagged his head. "True."

"No thanks."

Mr. Sharkawy scowled. "You could die down there."

I snorted. "Like I won't up there? I'll take my chances."

The museum director's face moved away, and I could hear him ordering his flunkies to fetch some rope. I wasn't worried. They couldn't catch me down here. I was safe.

I smiled.

And then, with a final crack, the floor gave way beneath me. Down I went.

Again.

Chapter Twenty

The Wonder Down Under

YOU'D THINK THAT falling through the floor into a tunnel would prepare you for doing it a second time. But you'd be wrong.

This time around, I landed in a shower of earth and bricks with a teeth-jarring *whump*. My elbow hurt, my hip hurt. Clouds of dust choked me. A steady flow of stink-water sprinkled me from above like the world's nastiest shower.

Hacking and coughing, I rolled off the rubble pile. I was bruised, I was dirty, but I wasn't hyena food. That was something.

Only the faintest glimmer of light reached down into this subtunnel—just enough to see that it, too, was brick-lined, but with a level floor. I strained my eyes peering both ways along the passage. Darkness and more darkness.

I took stock.

Here I was, somewhere underneath Monterrosa. Psycho Museum Guy and his crew were hunting for me above. Meanwhile, the afternoon sun was sinking, my teacher was only an hour or two away from going full-on were-hyena, I had lost my best friend, and I had no idea how to get myself, and the amulet, back up where we could do some good.

Not exactly a red-letter day.

I shouted, "Hello!" The word echoed on and on. No one answered, but it got me thinking about what else might be down here with me. That gave me the shivers, so I stopped calling out.

I shuffled down the tunnel in one direction, changed my mind, and headed the other way. Which path would take me to safety?

No clue.

Torn, I hesitated. Benny wouldn't hesitate. He'd just march off blindly without a second thought. I should be more like him—not in every way, maybe, but in his decisiveness. Heroes were decisive, after all.

I squared my shoulders and sucked in a deep breath. Okay, what would a hero do now? I wondered. What would Spider-Man do?

He'd pick a direction and swing off on his webbing, I told myself, *not stand around like a dope*. After a quick round of eeny, meeny, miny, moe, I chose the left-hand path. With my fingertips lightly brushing one wall, I stumbled forward, sweeping my free hand before me.

Every few steps, I paused and listened.

Odd gurgles, scuffling sounds, and mysterious muffled noises echoed along the passageway. But I couldn't tell if they were far or close, ahead or behind, or even what was causing them.

The darkness was absolute.

In fact, I could see no more with my eyes open than closed. Shuffling forward, I began to picture the creatures that shared this darkness with me. Hideous, lamp-eyed things like Gollum. Enormous, fanged were-moles. A race of mutant cannibals whose favorite dish was young boys.

After all, if were-hyenas walked above, who knew what monsters lived in the darkness beneath Monterrosa?

My heart knocked against my ribs like a pinball against a thumper bumper. My hands trembled.

Step-by-step, I shambled onward. More sounds came, but I couldn't tell if they were real or imaginary. Evil chuckles. Whooshes and creaks. The voices of lost souls muttering.

My fists clenched. A faint, eerie glow burned up ahead. I blinked. Was it an exit, or the source of more spookiness?

Abruptly, the tunnel veered right, and a bright light hit me in the face. Shadowy figures moved behind it.

"Die, mutant flesh eaters!" I screamed.

Blindly, I dashed forward with fists flailing, determined not to go down without a fight. My knuckles struck an arm, a chest, a flashlight. I tangled with a creature shorter than myself—a cannibal kid?

"Ow!" cried the flesh eater, and, "Quit it! Carlos, stop!"

It was the "Carlos" that got to me. That, and the fact that the cannibal's voice sounded familiar.

"Benny?" I said, lowering my fists.

He shone the flashlight in his own face. "The one and only," he confirmed.

I gripped his shoulders. A warm surge of relief welled up from my belly. "Oh, man, am I glad to see you!"

"I could tell." Benny rubbed his chest. "If you were any gladder, I'd have to go to the hospital."

"Are you all right, Carlos?" asked a woman's deep voice.

Shading my eyes against the glare, I asked, "Who's that?"

"Me." A quick flip of her head-mounted flashlight revealed Mrs. Tamasese in her tricked-out purple wheel-chair and orange hoodie. She grinned. "Trick or treat!"

I was floored. "But you . . ." I said to Benny. "But she . . ."

"Time's a-wasting," said Mrs. Tamasese.

"She's right," said Benny, grabbing my arm. "We'll explain on the way."

As we headed for the entrance, Benny filled me in on what had happened during my time in Wacko Museum Land. First, from Mrs. Tamasese he'd learned some vital info about alpha were-monsters—that they rule the pack, and that if you behead one, or neutralize it with an amulet, the whole pack will be freed from the curse. Then Benny had called the police station to check if I was still there. They, of course, had never seen me.

Thinking I'd gone back to school, he got Mrs. T to call the office, impersonating my mom. No luck there either.

With those options eliminated, Benny thought he knew where I'd be. He wanted the store owner to drive him there, but she had a better idea.

"Not many people know about these tunnels under the town," she said, wheeling alongside us. "Smugglers built 'em, back in the day. They connect lots of the older buildings."

I frowned. "But why look for me down here? I've never even heard about these tunnels before."

"I knew you'd go back to the museum eventually," said Benny. "You've got it in for that Sharkawy guy."

"Well, yeah," I said. "He's the head hyena for sure."

"So we had to figure out how to sneak in without him seeing us," said Benny.

Mrs. Tamasese cranked her wheels, easily keeping pace. "These tunnels access the museum's basement, so we planned to break in from there."

"A cop's son breaking and entering?" I said. "Has the world gone crazy? What's next, dogs marrying cats?"

"This." Benny popped a quick punch into my shoulder as a reply.

It was funny, but as we hurried along below street level, we were making much better time than we would have made up top. By the time I'd finished telling them what happened to me at the museum, we had reached a sturdy wooden door straight from an old-timey castle.

Mrs. Tamasese stopped her wheelchair. "They were going to sacrifice you?" she said, her brown face ashen in the spill of the flashlight.

"That's what Sharkawy said," I said.

"This is getting more *lolo* by the minute." Fishing out a set of keys, Mrs. Tamasese continued, "There's about an hour left before the moon rises and things get all hyena'd out. We'll have to move fast."

"'We'?" I said. "You're coming with us?"

The store owner unlocked and shoved open the door. Fluorescent lights from beyond revealed a grave expression on her face. "After what happened, I can't let you go alone."

"But your . . ." Benny gestured at her wheelchair.

"I may not be able to do everything, but at least I can do something," she said. "And this is no time to sit on the sidelines."

"I'm glad you're in the game with us," I said. And I was. I decided we had a better chance of success with her, an expert, than we did with the police. After all, I didn't want Mr. Chu getting arrested—or worse.

Mrs. Tamasese led the way into a basement corridor,

locking the door behind us. In no time at all, we bustled into an elevator, rose to the ground floor, and emerged from an old building two doors down from the comics store.

She rolled up to the front of her shop and reached for her keys.

"Um, if we're in a hurry," I said, "shouldn't we be, well, hurrying?"

A fierce smile lit Mrs. Tamasese's face. "When you're going up against were-creatures, you gotta be prepared. Hang loose, guys. I'll be right back."

Benny and I looked at each other, then down at the sidewalk. The silence stretched uncomfortably, full of things left unsaid.

"Before, I was . . ." I began.

"Yeah, me, too," said Benny.

I scratched my cheek. "And then . . ."

"I know," he said. "But . . ." He shrugged.

"Um, I never . . ."

He glanced over at me. "Me neither."

I screwed up my face and examined a cloud. "So . . ."

"So . . ." said Benny. He took a deep breath. "We good now?"

My eyes met his. "We're good."

We both smiled sheepishly, and he mock-punched my arm. With real friends, you don't need a whole lot of words.

Mrs. T emerged from her shop and handed each of us a necklace.

"More amulets?" I asked, patting the pocket where I'd stashed the one we'd stolen from the museum.

"You might say that," said Mrs. T.

I examined the necklace she'd given me more closely. From my chain dangled a figure that looked suspiciously like a Pokémon character.

"Silver," she said. "Wear it around your neck—shapeshifters hate the silver."

"But, Pikachu?" I said doubtfully.

"Silver is silver," she said. "Plus, it's a collectible."

We donned our protective Pokémon necklaces and took a mysterious pet carrier from her. Mrs. Tamasese's van waited behind the building. Much like her wheelchair, it was, as she said, a sweet ride. Custom-painted in purple, blue, and gold, it featured the words SAMOAN STRONG arching over a wave.

At a press of her key fob, the van chirped, a side door slid open, and a ramp unfolded.

"Cool," Benny and I breathed together.

Once inside, Mrs. Tamasese locked her wheelchair into place where the driver's seat would've been and worked a series of levers, knobs, and electronic controls that would've put the bridge of the starship *Enterprise* to shame.

The engine revved like an Indy 500 racecar.

"Buckle up, boys," she said. "It's gonna be a bumpy night."

Chapter Twenty-One

Graveheart

OUR FIRST big challenge? We didn't know where to go. After all, the were-hyenas didn't exactly have a Hyena Haven clubhouse where we could find them anytime, laughing like loonies and snacking on carrion. The museum was definitely out—Mr. Sharkawy and his flunkies would have to find a new sacrifice.

After discussing it, Benny and I decided something. Since Mr. Chu had been bitten out by the graveyard, and Benny's dad had told him this morning that more graves had been dug up, and we'd seen our first were-hyena at the graveyard, our best bet was—major duh—the graveyard.

As we motored out of town in Mrs. Tamasese's van, I checked the sun. It peeked between charcoal clouds, as fat and golden as a low-hanging grapefruit.

I shivered. We had maybe half an hour before moonrise.

My stomach growled for its missed dinner. I ignored it. I was too keyed up to eat anyway.

Benny's phone rang. From his first few responses, I figured it was his mom, wondering where he was. He put the call on speakerphone.

"—and just because we haven't told you yet doesn't mean you're not grounded," said Mrs. Brackman. "Come home right now!"

"Um, I can't," said Benny.

"What do you mean? Of course you can. Your father won't like this."

He glanced over. "We're . . . doing something important for school, Carlos and me. It's for Mr. Chu."

Yeah, we're trying to stop him from becoming a raving werecreature, I added silently.

"Hi, Mrs. Brackman," I said sheepishly.

"Carlos, your grandma has been looking for you," Benny's mom said. "And she's not happy."

I grimaced. "Tell her I'll be home as soon as this project is over?" I asked. "And that I'm sorry."

"I'm not your messenger," said Mrs. Brackman.

"Please?" I asked. "As a favor?"

The sound of a sigh came over the phone. "All right," she said. "Oh, and boys? I got an urgent call from Tina Green's mother."

"Really?" Benny said. "What about?"

Mrs. Brackman's voice sounded worried. "Tina didn't

come home from school. And she had told a friend that she would be doing something involving you two."

"Us?" I said. Benny and I stared at the phone as if it could clear up the mystery. I felt a pang of guilt that I'd completely forgotten my promise to include her in the big finale with the were-hyenas. On the other hand, she'd be much safer out of the action.

"She's not with you now, is she?" asked Mrs. Brackman.

"Uh, no," I said. "But she's, uh . . ."

"She's working on the same project as us," said Benny. "When we see her, we'll tell her to call home." And that wasn't even a total lie.

Benny's mom said good-bye. But not before making us promise to keep a positive outlook, make good choices, and come home for grounding right after our project was over.

Telling her we'd be happy to, unless were-hyenas gobbled us up, fell under the category of Things Mothers Don't Need to Know. So we promised we'd be home as soon as we could. Benny hung up.

"You don't think Tina went sniffing around those wackos at the museum?" I said. My throat felt tight at the thought of her falling into Mr. Sharkawy's clutches.

"I sure hope not," said Mrs. Tamasese. "She seems like a nice girl, and she's got a terrific collection of Wonder Woman comic books—one of the best."

"Tina's smart," said Benny. "She'll stay out of trouble."

But I wasn't too sure. I kept remembering how eager she'd been to cure Mr. Chu of his problem. Could she have gotten into trouble with the were-hyenas?

I borrowed Benny's phone to call her. The call went to voice mail.

Then we turned onto Oswald Road, and all thoughts of Tina fled from my head. The closer we got, the more my stomach bubbled like posole stew. As the van approached the cemetery access road, Mrs. Tamasese said, "You boys sure you want to do this?"

I looked down at my hands. "We have to. If we don't step up—"

"Nobody will," Benny finished.

The former wrestler nodded. "Okay, then. Look, I can only go so far. This old graveyard"—she gave a bitter smile—"isn't exactly wheelchair-friendly. But I'll keep watch, and if things get too hairy, I'll call for backup."

"Hairy," said Benny. "Hyenas. I get it. Heh." But his humor sounded forced.

The shadows of the oak trees stretched long dark fingers across the road. The sun raced toward the horizon, and I could feel the full moon waiting to burst over the hill like a huge rotten egg.

My limbs tingled. I felt thirsty. I wished I was at my own kitchen table with a huge mug of hot chocolate.

At the end of the road, Mrs. Tamasese turned her van

around and parked. "Remember, I'm your wheelman," she said. "If things get *kapakahi*—"

"Cup of coffee?" said Benny.

"Messed up," said the former wrestler. "As soon as the situation goes south, make a run for the van. Now, what did I tell you about those were-creatures?"

"Get to the alpha before he changes, if we can," said Benny.

"Watch out after they change, because they're superfast and strong," I said.

"And above all . . ." said Benny.

"Don't get bitten," we said together. My voice trembled, despite our bravado. I hoped Benny hadn't noticed.

Satisfied, Mrs. Tamasese nodded. "Carlos, you got your amulet?" I patted my pocket. Mrs. T turned and gestured at the mysterious carrier we'd stashed in the van for her. "I almost forgot. Take Honey Girl with you."

"Honey Girl?" asked Benny, picking up the container.

I slid back the cover to reveal a fat, fluffy calico cat. *Mmmrow*, said Honey Girl.

"Cats can sense the supernatural," said Mrs. T. "Plus she might act as bait."

My eyebrows climbed my forehead. "Really? You'd risk your cat with those monsters?"

She snorted. "The risk is all on their side. Honey Girl can handle herself."

Although I had my doubts, we took the carrier with us when we left the van.

"Good luck, boys," Mrs. Tamasese called. "Give 'um!" And she flashed us a Hawaiian "hang loose" sign.

Great, I thought. We're facing off against a pack of homicidal hyena-men, armed only with two Pokémon necklaces and a chubby cat. No worries there.

Benny and I crunched along the narrow gravel pathway between the headstones, the dying sun throwing monstrous shadows behind us. The hillside lay quiet, except for a lone bird's nervous twitters. We reached a fork in the path.

"Let's head back to where we were last night," said Benny.

I was about to agree, like always, but then I got a strong prickly feeling, almost like Peter Parker's Spidey sense. "No," I said slowly. "Let's go up by the crypts. That's where they'll be."

"But it makes more sense to—" Benny cut himself off, looked up at me, and nodded. "You know what, let's go to the crypts."

I smiled.

We headed up the hill to where all the dead rich people were buried. A miniature city of fancy little granite homes for corpses, the mausoleums were lousy with Greek pillars and angel statues. In the fading light, some of the angels looked ready to hop off their pedestals and head home.

I knew how they felt. My legs quivered like a hoot owl's wings in a hurricane.

When I glanced at Benny, I noticed his teeth were clenched in a skeleton's smile and his fists were knotted. Were we both crazy?

Duh. Why else would we be there?

As we approached the first crypt, the wind shifted, carrying the sound of voices. Benny and I ducked behind the stone structure.

Ever so carefully, we peeked around the side. I caught my breath.

Just up the hill, in a clearing between crypts, someone had set up four bright Coleman lanterns on tombstones. In the space between, that same someone had carved a wide circle into the grass, with a five-pointed star inside.

Equally spaced around the circle stood four people: Snake Woman and Mr. Stretch from the museum; the alpha hyena himself, Mr. Sharkawy; and my mom's hairdresser, Mrs. Macadangdang.

But inside the circle stood something that shook me worst of all:

Gagged, groggy, and tied to a post was our very own Karate Girl, Tina Green.

Chapter Twenty-Two

Angry Nerds

BENNY'S HAND gripped my shoulder. "We've gotta get her out of there!"

Suddenly my fear evaporated like a milk shake on Mercury. "Oh, yeah," I whispered. "We will. Preferably without being sacrificed ourselves."

"Any ideas?"

I glanced at the rapidly setting sun. "Let the cat out."

Benny gave me a funny look.

"It's almost moonrise," I said, "and she'll make sure we have advance warning before things get supernatural. Plus, it's not fair to leave her in there."

"All right," he whispered. "Loose the Honey Girl!"

I opened the carrier door. The big calico scampered out, sat down, and promptly began licking her butt.

"That's a big help," said Benny. "Any other thoughts?"

I gnawed my lip. "You know, if I can just hang this

amulet around Mr. Sharkawy's neck, all our troubles are over."

He grinned. "I'll distract him, you jump him."

I wished we had a better plan than that, but our time was almost up. I nodded. "Give me a minute to get into position, then lure him over by that crypt." I indicated a smaller mausoleum off to the right.

"Why that one?" asked Benny. "Good supernatural juju?"

I shook my head. "Short enough for me to climb onto."

We bumped fists for luck, and then I crept in a wide circle, ducking from tombstone to tombstone like a grave-yard ninja. I needn't have bothered. The museum director's hyena crew stayed totally focused on their sinister ritual.

Mr. Sharkawy recited words from a yellowed scroll, which his Sharkettes echoed. "We call upon the four directions—north, west, east, and south. . . ."

"North, west, east, south," his flunkies repeated in a reciting-the-Pledge-of-Allegiance tone.

"We call upon the spirit of the full moon, which rises. . . ."

"The full moon rises," chanted the Sharkettes.

Tina stirred, raising her head. Her eyes got huge. "Gnngh!" she said through the gag, and struggled against her bonds.

By then, I had reached the little crypt, which was built into the hillside like a hobbit house. Sneaking around back, I climbed onto its roof, staying low.

The sun sank halfway behind the horizon. Then . . .

"Hello there, ladies and germs!" Benny boomed, stepping into the open. "And welcome to Weirdo-Palooza! I can see the weirdos are already out in force."

"You insolent boy!" snarled Mr. Sharkawy.

"That's my name," said Benny. "Don't wear it out."

The Sharkettes gawked in disbelief.

"Hi, Mrs. Macadangdang," said Benny. "What are you doing here?"

The hairdresser automatically raised a hand in greeting. "I, uh . . . like animals?" she said uncertainly.

"Gngh mff!" grunted Tina.

Mr. Sharkawy pointed off dramatically. "Leave us, boy!" he thundered. "You profane our holy ritual with your presence."

Benny began angling in my direction. "Hey, you turn my stomach with your ugly face," he said, "but you don't hear me complaining."

I grinned. Score one for Benny. No one did irritating better than him.

With a glance at the setting sun, Mr. Sharkawy snapped, "Go, now!"

"Gee, I think I'll stay," said Benny. "No place nicer than a graveyard at sundown. So peaceful."

"Then our animal ancestors will enjoy a second sacrifice," said the museum director. "Mr. Nutters, seize him!"

The freakishly tall Mr. Nutters left the circle, spread his

freakishly long arms, and rushed after Benny. He snatched, and came up with nothing but air. Grunting in frustration, he grabbed again, and once more Benny spun away.

Apparently, Mr. Nutters didn't know that Benny was the two-time dodgeball champion of our grade. My friend had some serious moves.

But all his juking and jiving didn't get me any closer to playing ring toss on Mr. Sharkawy. I drew the amulet from my pocket. It felt warm.

"Hold still!" Mr. Nutters barked, lunging again. Benny ducked around a tombstone, making the tall man bang his knee hard and do a face-plant in the grass.

The museum director blew out a sigh. "Must I do everything myself?" Apparently, the answer was yes, because he set down his scroll and ran at Benny.

That's the stuff, I thought. Just a little closer . . .

Benny slipped Mr. Sharkawy's grab and darted past my crypt. Much faster than his too-tall flunky, the museum director followed, hard on his heels.

I gathered myself and sprang.

As I jumped, I noticed two things from the corner of my eye: (a) Tina Green leaping up and down, trying to slip her bound hands off the post; and (b) the last red sliver of sun sinking into the ocean.

Moonrise.

My timing was as perfect as if we'd rehearsed it.

Just as Mr. Sharkawy passed my crypt, I hit him from

behind like a load of bricks. Down he went, face-first. But my hand was empty.

Where was the amulet?

Kneeling on his back, I scrabbled around for the necklace, which had flown free at impact. I only had seconds before he went all hyenoid and scarfed me down like Carlos niblets.

My hands shook. It felt like I was holding back a scream.

The museum director writhed underneath me. Was he beginning to change? I gripped tighter with my knees.

"Ow, that hurts!" he said into the dirt.

There! At last my hands closed on the amulet's heavy chain. But with a sudden twist, Mr. Sharkawy threw me off his back. He climbed to one knee.

Before he could stand, I surged forward and slipped the ancient charm around his neck. Just as I did, a huge hand closed around my upper arm.

"Gotcha!" Mr. Nutters had me.

The museum director rose to his feet, lifting the amulet and blinking at it in surprise.

"Ha!" I crowed. "Suck on that, hyena face!"

Mr. Sharkawy stared at the necklace in the light of the lanterns. A strange look crept across his features. "So you brats *did* steal it after all."

It was my turn to stare. The moon had risen over the hill, as full and fat as a big old lemon pie. Yet here was the alpha hyena, examining the amulet with a satisfied sneer.

What about the writhing in agony? The turning into a puddle of goo?

"Die, twisted fiend!" I cried.

But he didn't die. Mr. Sharkawy let the talisman fall back against his chest. "Thanks for returning this," he said. "But we're still going to sacrifice you. Bring him," he told Mr. Nutters.

I thrashed about. "No!"

And then, a bloodcurdling caterwaul froze us all in our tracks:

Rrrreeeauh!

Craning around, I spotted Honey Girl crouched by a gravestone with all her fur standing on end. Something was setting off the cat.

And I thought I knew what.

From someplace close, an eerie cry split the twilight. *"Eeee-heh-heh-heh-heh!"*

My legs went rubbery.

The *real* were-hyena had arrived!

Chapter Twenty-Three

Hyena and Mighty

I T STALKED AROUND the side of the hill, threading its way between tombstones. Silhouetted against the full moon, its shape came into sharp relief. Brawny shoulders. Shaggy head. Long pointed ears, and long arms tipped with claws.

The were-hyena gave a low chuckle, and my insides turned to guacamole.

"Guh," I said.

Mr. Nutters's hand slipped off my arm. He took a step back. The two women sidled away from their circle. But not Mr. Sharkawy.

His face wore a look of awed terror. Slowly he sank to his knees and raised his arms. "We salute you, sacred one who holds the secrets of the night," he said.

Growling, the were-hyena prowled closer. Lantern light gleamed off its sharp teeth and crazed eyes, picking out a whitish blaze on the left side of its chest.

My jaw dropped. *This* was the alpha, not Mr. Sharkawy.

"Behold," said the museum director, indicating Tina and the circle. "We bring you a sacrifice, that you may look upon us and be pleased. Grant us your dark gift."

I spared a second for a glance around. The Sharkettes seemed less keen on the dark gift than Mr. Sharkawy; they kept backing away from the circle, faces slack with dread. Tina was hurling her body back and forth against the metal post, trying to tear it from the ground.

And Benny?

A voice muttered near my ear, "We had the wrong alpha."

"Looks like," I told him. "You help Tina, I'll get the amulet back."

But before we could move, we heard another *"Eeee-heh-heh-heh!"* from behind us. It was answered by a third insane giggle from off to our left.

Surrounded.

I'd been scared so many times the past day or so, I figured I'd reached my terror limit. But I was wrong. At that very moment, I was petrified to the max. But somehow I forced my feet to move.

"Welcome!" Mr. Sharkawy brayed, still on his knees. "Welcome, ancient ones! Bring us your beast magic!"

And he was still babbling whacked-out stuff like that when I stepped up behind him, snagged the chain, and lifted the amulet off his neck. It caught on his beaky nose. When the museum director clutched the medallion, I thought I'd lost it for good.

But then I jabbed my fingers into his armpit—a tickling technique that always works on my little sister—and Mr. Sharkawy lost his grip.

The amulet was mine.

Only one problem: now the alpha hyena had me in its sights. It stalked forward, rumbling like a vindictive volcano, mad eyes fixed on me.

I scurried backward and tripped over a gravestone, falling to my knees. The necklace burned in my hand. I had no idea how to get it around the monster's throat—and the were-hyena clearly wasn't about to bow down and make it easy for me.

The monster raised its arms, looming. Then it recoiled, a look of almost human revulsion crossing its face.

Fssshht! With back arched and hiss dialed up to eleven, Honey Girl appeared directly in the monster's path. The crazy cat was taking on a were-hyena!

"Go, Honey Girl!" I cried, rising to my feet.

For a few long seconds, it looked like a standoff. Then both creatures seemed to realize that the monster was about ten times taller than the house cat. The were-hyena snarled and stamped its foot, and Honey Girl scooted behind a crypt, leaving me exposed.

"No Meow Mix for you," I muttered.

"Move it!' cried Tina.

I dodged around a tombstone, clutching the amulet. A glance behind showed me both good news and bad news. The good: Tina was free. The bad: Were-hyenas Two and Three had closed in on us, blocking off any retreat. Tongues lolling, they drooled like we were fresh tamales on a plate. The Sharkettes huddled together by a crypt, watching the creatures with huge, panicked eyes.

My attention stayed riveted on the alpha hyena.

"Hey, Benny?" I called over my shoulder.

"Yeah?"

"Any ideas?"

His voice sounded high and tight. "Sure. Rule Number Three: don't get bitten."

"I'll try to remember that," I said.

At this point, Mr. Sharkawy noticed that his sacrificial offering had gotten loose. Glowering, he told the monster, "The unbelievers are trying to escape. I offer all of them as your sacrifice. Take them!"

"Go ahead and try," said Tina, settling into her fiercest karate stance. But her voice wobbled.

The alpha hyena swung its shaggy head from her and Benny, back to me.

"*They're* the tasty ones," I blurted. "Not me." (It wasn't my proudest moment.)

Maybe the monster didn't really understand English, or maybe it just had its mouth set for a yummy Carlos snack. With a low grunt, the were-hyena gathered itself and sprang straight at me—a twenty-foot leap, like a killer kangaroo.

Oh, shoot.

"Yaahh!" I ducked behind a gravestone and prayed, but I knew it was no use. I'd be shredded like a cheap cabbage. My last thought was a silent apology to my dad for breaking my curfew and dying.

But the monster didn't kill me.

"Grrraaahh!" A blur of darkness flew across the moon as someone or some*thing* else struck the alpha in midair.

Two bodies dropped, tumbling over and over as the creatures bit and scratched and fought.

"No!" cried Mr. Sharkawy. He edged forward and backward, not quite brave enough to jump in and help his monster buddy.

When the brawlers rolled into the lantern light, I could see the attacker more clearly. It was a new monster, but this was no ordinary were-hyena. He was wearing Hello Kitty boxer shorts.

"Mr. Chu?!" I said.

"Knock his block off!" Benny urged our were-teacher.

First, one monster had the advantage, and then the

other did. With a howl, the Mr. Chu hyena heaved the alpha onto its back, knocking the wind out of it. The other shapeshifters whined and jittered about, but they kept their distance.

The Chu-monster got his hands around the alpha's neck and began to choke. The alpha fought back, twisting and clawing.

"Go, Mr. Chu!" cried Tina. She and Benny had drifted over to join me.

At the sound of his name, the Chu-monster turned his head toward us. And that's when the alpha struck. With a roar, it broke our teacher's grip, bucked, and flung him aside.

Mr. Chu's head hit a grave marker with a sickening crunch. He twitched and lay still.

"No! Mr. Chu!" My heart sank into my shoes. Was he dead? Had we gotten in this much trouble, this much danger, only to lose the man we were trying to save? Tears welled.

The alpha hyena rested one clawed foot on Mr. Chu's chest, raised its monstrous head, and ripped out a chilling laugh. The other hyenas echoed it.

Then the eyes of all three creatures landed on us.

"Ulp," said Benny.

"What now?" said Tina.

I sucked in a deep breath, trying to calm my panic. "I've got a terrible idea, but it just might work. Table Topple."

Tina said, "You're right, that is a terrible idea."

The hyenas held a brief chuckle conversation—probably deciding who got to eat whom.

"But you're our black belt Karate Girl," I said, keeping an eye on their monster huddle. "You can handle it, right?"

Tina's brown eyes glittered in the lantern glow. "Heh. Funny thing—I haven't actually taken any classes."

Benny's forehead crinkled. "But all your karate moves?"

"Learned 'em from Jackie Chan movies," said Tina.

"They look so real," I said.

She offered an apologetic smile. "It's mostly attitude. If you act like you know what you're doing, people tend to believe you."

Conversation over, the alpha rumbled deep in its chest and stalked toward us. Its lips peeled back from a major mouthful of sharp teeth.

"Then this would be a good time to act," I said. I jerked my head to one side. "Go, Benny. Be the table. We've got this."

Tina and I split up, one to the left, one to the right. I held the amulet ready. And as Benny slipped behind a crypt, we waved our arms about and did what we did best— trash-talking the alpha were-hyena.

"You're so ugly, they're thinking about moving Halloween to your birthday!" Tina shouted.

The monster snarled and turned toward her.

"You call those teeth?" I yelled. "I've seen sharper teeth on a comb!"

The were-hyena shifted its growl to me. All my limbs went shaky.

Tina waved her arms. "You listening to me, bat ears? You're so ugly, you can sink your face in dough and make monster cookies."

"Don't insult the ancient one!" cried Mr. Sharkawy from his safe spot over by the Sharkettes. He didn't notice, but I glimpsed a crouched figure creeping toward the were-hyena from behind. Benny was almost in position.

When the alpha whirled on Tina, I distracted it with one last insult. "Your mama's so hairy, when your grandma gave birth to her, she got rug burn!"

That did it. No matter what species you are, human or were-creature or fuzzy wombat, you do *not* insult someone's mama.

With a roar like a sonic boom, the monster turned its six-feet-plus of fangs, claws, menace, and muscle on me.

I was dead meat.

Chapter Twenty-Four

Nude Awakening

AS THE WERE-HYENA raised its beefy arms to shred me to ribbons, Benny and Tina pulled the Table Topple, a playground trick so old, kids must have been doing it since Pharaoh was in diapers.

On hands and knees, Benny planted himself directly behind the monster. Then, with a loud "Heeee-*yah*!" Tina drove straight at the distracted were-hyena, leaping into the air to deliver her best Bruce Lee karate kick.

The monster had just enough time to widen its eyes in disbelief.

Wham! Tina's feet slammed into its chest. The alpha hyena staggered, the backs of its knees hit Benny's body, and *whump!*—down it went.

Before it could recover, I rushed in close and slipped the amulet around that hairy neck.

Two powerful hands reached up and caught my shoulders in an unbreakable grip. I struggled, but those hands drew me down, down, toward the scariest face I'd ever seen, all fangs and wild eyes and nightmare bad breath.

"No!" I cried.

My Pikachu necklace swung free. The creature hissed at the silver dangling in its face. But it didn't stop pulling me.

I braced my hands against the monster's chest, resisting. No use.

The were-hyena's jaws opened wide. . . .

And then the amulet began to sizzle on that chest like a skillet frying bacon. With an unearthly moan, the monster released me to scrabble at its own breast. But the amulet wouldn't budge.

It was fused to the skin.

The other were-hyenas howled. Benny, Tina, and I scrambled back, horrified and fascinated.

Bucking, thrashing, and writhing on the ground, the creature made every sound in its vocabulary, from whines and moans to grunts and giggles. An awful smell, like burned dog hairs and vomit and putrid flesh all rolled into one, rose from its body.

The amulet glowed electric blue.

And then, with a full-body shudder, the monster twitched one last time and fell still. Under our gaze, the brawny body began to shrink. The whole scene was like

one of those time-lapse nature shows about a plant growing, but in reverse.

The ears shriveled back into the head. The spotted fur
retracted into the body. The muscles withered, the snout
telescoped, and in less than a minute, the monstrous form
turned into . . .

A woman.

"Oh!" cried Benny, throwing up a hand and turning
away.

A naked woman.

"Is that . . . ?" breathed Tina.

A naked woman known as . . .

"Ms. Icaza?" I said. "*She's* the alpha?"

Tina peeled off her jacket and draped it over the uncon-
scious museum worker. "What?" she said to me, bristling.
"Like a strong woman can't be a leader?"

"No, no," I said, holding up my palms. "A woman has
just as much right as a man to lead a pack of homicidal,
half-monster freaks."

"You got that right," said Tina.

Things went a little blurry after that. I felt so dizzy, I had
to sit down on a grave marker until the feeling passed. Mrs.
Tamasese must have called the police, because, next thing I
knew, cops and paramedics were swarming the hillside like
ants on an abandoned piñata.

"There they are!" yelled a tall policewoman. "Don't let the cult members escape!"

"Got 'em, Lieutenant!" Three cops surrounded Mr. Sharkawy and his Sharkettes. The museum director wouldn't be receiving his "dark gift" after all—unless it was an all-expenses-paid trip to prison.

The paramedics loaded Ms. Icaza and Mr. Chu onto stretchers. I was relieved to see that our teacher was stirring. Then the cops herded everyone else over to the parking lot, including two naked and confused people—the other two former were-hyenas. Mrs. Tamasese drove up in her van, tooting the horn and grinning as wide as the Pacific Ocean.

As the ex-wrestler opened the side door and rolled her way over to us, I asked Tina, "So how'd you get caught by Mr. Sharkawy and his loonies?"

She punched my arm. "It's your fault," she said.

"Mine?"

"I was hustling around on my bike, trying to find you guys," said Tina. "On a hunch, I went by the museum, and just outside it, I found this." She unfolded a sheet of paper from her pocket, and I recognized one of the HELP! notes I'd scrawled when Mr. Sharkawy had me locked up.

"Ohhh," I said.

"Yeah, 'ohhh,'" she said. "When I tried to sneak in and bust you out, they caught me."

I offered her an apologetic smile. "Sorry."

Tina only grunted.

And then it sank in that she had risked her life to save me. "Um, thanks," I said.

"For what?"

I coughed. "You stuck out your neck for me."

Tina snorted. "Like you did for me. Don't get all soppy, Rivera. That's what friends do."

My chest seemed to expand then, like I'd sucked in a tank of helium. A smile tugged at the corners of my mouth. Friends, huh? I could do a lot worse.

Mrs. Tamasese gave us all warm hugs. After telling us how worried she'd been, she praised our monster-busting technique to the skies. "I knew you could do it! After I called the cops, I caught your tag-team takedown through binoculars." She wagged her head. "Ho! You kids could have a bright future in professional wrestling."

Then Mrs. T pulled the tall policewoman aside and spun her a story of courageous kids taking down a deranged cult. Her comic-book experience really paid off. I nearly believed it myself.

Past the two of them, a dark sedan pulled into the lot, and the last person I expected to see got out of it.

"Hey," said Benny. "Isn't that our sub?"

His scowl as deep as the Grand Canyon, Mr. Kardoz stomped over to the ambulance, where the paramedics were about to load in Mr. Chu and Ms. Icaza.

"Stop!" he yelled. "Hold it right there!"

Curious, we hustled over to see what was going on.

Two of the blue-uniformed policemen blocked Mr. Kardoz from the patients on gurneys. Mr. Sharkawy and his Sharkettes stood nearby in handcuffs, looking on.

"What's the beef?" asked one burly cop.

Our substitute reached into the pocket of his sports coat and withdrew a small leather wallet with some kind of shiny badge attached. "Special Agent Kardoz," he said. "FBI Art Crimes Unit."

"Yeah?" said the cop.

"Yeah," said the sub. "And I am taking that woman into custody."

Benny and I exchanged glances.

"Art crimes?" he said.

"FBI?" I said.

"That explains a lot of things."

The husky policeman squinted at Mr. Kardoz's badge, then at the dazed Ms. Icaza. "What'd she do?" he asked.

"Stole a bunch of priceless African art," Agent Kardoz growled. "I have followed her for days, tapped her phone. She was planning on selling everything to a fence for big bucks."

The cop whistled, impressed.

Mr. Sharkawy tugged away from his captors and approached his employee's gurney. "Stolen?" he said, his face pasty. "You told me you acquired the collection with help from an anonymous benefactor."

A groggy Ms. Icaza rolled her head to look at him. "I lied."

"And the tour of other museums? All the plans for this exhibit?"

"All lies." The former were-hyena seemed tired and grayer than before.

Veins stood out in Mr. Sharkawy's forehead. "You . . . you . . ."

"And I would've gotten away with it, too," said Ms. Icaza bitterly, "if that stupid creature hadn't bitten me during our Lagos heist. Who uses hyenas as watchdogs?"

"Aw, poor baby," Mrs. Tamasese said sarcastically.

"Wait," said Benny, "you got bit by a hyena?"

"No, I run around cackling in the moonlight for my health," she said. "Yes, I was bitten."

I nodded. "So you must have changed into a were-hyena at the first full moon after you returned. And then you bit other people."

Ms. Icaza started to answer, then glanced at the FBI agent. "Something like that. It's all a blur."

"Well, your hyena days are over," I told her.

She sighed. "Just as well. I was getting tired of eating corpses anyway."

Benny, Tina, and I did a simultaneous "Eeeww."

As Mr. Kardoz handcuffed Ms. Icaza to the gurney, the museum director pushed up beside her again. He looked like a second grader who's just learned that the Easter Bunny is really his aunt Lulu in a rabbit costume.

"And the animal magic? The amulets, the rituals?" he quavered. "I suppose all that was a lie, too?"

Ms. Icaza rolled her eyes. "Grow up, David. Everyone knows magic isn't real."

Mrs. Tamasese smirked.

The paramedics loaded Ms. Icaza and Mr. Chu into the ambulance. I glanced over at Benny. Maybe what we'd seen tonight wasn't make-a-Buick-disappear-into-a-hankie kind of magic, but it sure as heck wasn't normal.

Benny shrugged. "I guess you see what you want to see," he said.

"For reals," said Mrs. Tamasese.

But the fun wasn't quite over yet. Two more cars pulled into the parking lot, and Benny's dad and my dad hurried over to us. We each got a big hug.

"We're so glad you're safe," said Mr. Brackman. "I heard all about the cult on the scanner, and how you helped break it up. Is it true they had trained bears?"

"Big ones," said Benny.

"You were both so brave," said my dad. Warmth radiated through my chest at his words.

Benny's eyes met mine. His expression said, *Hey, if that's what they want to believe* . . .

"We're just glad it's over," I said. And I meant it.

Benny shook his head. "What a night."

"We love you boys," said my dad.

Aww. "Love you, too, Dad," I said.

"And you should both know," said Mr. Brackman gently, "that you're grounded for a month."

Chapter Twenty-Five

Welcome to Monstertown

THE TRUTH IS a slippery beast. Tina, Benny, and I stuck to Mrs. Tamasese's "cult" story. I have no idea what the Sharkettes told the cops about what went on that night. I only know that no were-hyena reports turned up on the TV news.

For several days afterward, the "bear" attacks, Satanists in the graveyard, and African art theft were all that anyone in Monterrosa talked about.

Both Mr. Sharkawy and Ms. Icaza were arrested and thrown in jail. The Sharkettes got off with a fine and community service, after they paid for re-sodding the graveyard's grass. And those two confused nudists, the other were-hyenas? They had only the blurriest of memories from their time in monster form. Since no crimes could be pinned to them other than indecent exposure, they were fined and released.

To our great relief, Mr. Chu recovered quickly from his concussion and various scratches. He maintained that he'd gotten some kind of weird fever from his dog bite, which was why he couldn't recall the showdown in the cemetery. We let him believe that. It was probably better that way.

Maybe Benny was right—you see what you want to see, and you hear what you want to hear.

None of our parents would have believed what really happened anyway. Not even Benny's dad, who is an actual police detective and has seen plenty of weird stuff in his time.

After a few days, life began getting back to normal. (Or what passes for normal in Monterrosa.) Mr. Chu went totally bald again and threw himself back into teaching with his usual enthusiasm. His assignment to report on "seeing things from an animal's point of view" was particularly thought-provoking.

One day Benny and I returned early from recess and caught him bent over his trash can, sniffing wistfully. "Oh! Hi, boys," he said, straightening.

"Hey, Mr. Chu," we answered.

A dark cloud seemed to cross his face. "The, uh, other day . . . when I had that fever . . ."

"Yeah?" said Benny.

"You didn't see—I mean, I didn't do anything . . ."

"Strange and disturbing?" I said.

"Well, yeah," he said.

We shook our heads. "No way," said Benny.

I gave our teacher a considering look. "Although I do have to ask," I said, "are you by any chance a fan of Hello Kitty?"

Funny, but I never knew someone could blush all the way to the top of their head before.

Tina began hanging out more with Benny and me—not in a cootie-producing way, just in a friendly way. She dubbed the three of us the "hyena-busters," and began showing Benny and me some of her karate moves.

At home, we started getting used to our new situation. My abuela moved in—just on weekdays—to help take care of me while Mom and Veronica were off doing their Hollywood thing.

Our first weekend dinner together as a family was a lively one. My junior diva sister barely shut up enough to eat.

"You totally won't believe who I met our first week of taping," said Veronica. She rattled off the names of several actors I'd never heard of. "And I got autographs, and a swag bag, and a dressing room in pink, and the director even gave me a giant stuffed bear!"

"That's nice," I said.

For once, my mom didn't hang on my sister's every word.

She reached over and touched my hand. "Your father tells me you had some experiences with bears, too."

"Um, yeah," I said. "But not the cuddly kind."

Her eyes grew round. "You boys were so courageous. When I think about the danger you were in"—she put a hand to her chest—"it gives me the shudders."

My face got warm. "Oh, well, you know . . ."

"I think my brave boy deserves another slice of cake," said my mother.

I grinned. The look on Veronica's face was priceless.

Yes, life was back on an even keel. But with a *slight* change.

Things were different at home—better. And somehow, I didn't feel quite the same as before. Maybe almost getting munched by a savage were-hyena changes you. One thing for sure, I found that I have friends I can rely on no matter how weird things get. And I learned that even a nerd kid can find the strength to stand up to monsters.

That stuff stays with you. Right?

I sure hoped so. Because, only a week after the grave-yard incident, I got the feeling I might need to use what I'd learned, and soon.

Benny had gotten a pass from his grounding to come over and join the three of us for dinner. Abuelita had gone all festive, making chicken tamales with rice and beans, and Benny's favorite pumpkin empanadas.

I had just told him a goofy story from my little sister's first week in Hollywood, and we were loading up on seconds. Then my dad chuckled, half to himself.

"What is it, Mr. Rivera?" asked Benny.

Dad wagged his head. "Oh, nothing. Just this loony at work."

"Why? What'd he do?" I asked, forking another empanada onto my plate.

My dad pushed his glasses up the bridge of his nose with a finger. His eyes twinkled. "Well, this guy claims that he was out walking last night and saw a neighbor's dog get carried off by a bat."

"Pretty wacky," I said. Benny gave me a look.

"Oh, that's not the strangest part." My dad leaned onto his elbows. "This nut claims that the bat was the size of a Great Dane, and that it had the claws of an eagle and the head of a panther." He chuckled again. "That's as crazy as that Halloween story you boys told me about were-hyenas. Can you believe it?"

"Yeah," I said. "I can." I gave Benny a look.

And right then, we both knew. Things in Monterrosa were going to get a lot weirder before they got normal.

LOOK FOR BOOK **2** IN THE
MONSTERTOWN MYSTERY SERIES:

HOW WELL DO YOU KNOW the staff at your school? Sure, they bandage your scrapes, sweep up your spills, and dish out your lunch. But who are they, *really*?

They seem like nice people.

But what if they're not?

What if they're secretly something much, much weirder?

Thanks to this suspicion, Benny Brackman and I found ourselves in the school kitchen one night, cowering behind a refrigerator door.

"*¡Ay, huey!*" I gasped. "What the heck was that?"

Benny peeked around the door toward the pantry in the corner. Nothing moved in the dimness.

"Don't ask me, Carlos," he said. "All I saw was you, running like mad. What did you see?"

"Freakity freaking freakiness!" I said. My heart hammered like a tree full of woodpeckers and my nerves jangled like wind chimes in a hurricane.

"Can you be more specific?" Benny asked, squinting into the dark.

"Too many arms, scary fast, and it nearly took my head off. Where'd it go?"

I peered around Benny's shoulder. Although the open fridge did supply some yellowish light, its door faced the wrong way, back toward the deep fryer. My eyes were dazzled by brightness, which made the corner where the creature had ambushed me seem even darker.

"We should make sure what it is," whispered Benny.

"*You* make sure," I said. "That thing doesn't want us investigating the pantry, and I'm inclined to agree with it." Sweat popped out on my forehead.

Benny grumbled, but he gave in. We stared at the dark corner; we stared at the exit. All was quiet. Whatever it might be, the monster was motionless.

"Okay," I said, my throat dry, "we should go."

"You first," said Benny.

"No, you," I said. "I insist."

Benny licked his lips, and said, "Let's go together."

"Right."

The only problem with this plan was that the path to the exit ran much too close to the murky corner for comfort. My jaw clenched.

Nothing to it but to do it. My muscles tensed tighter than piano strings.

"On the count of three," said Benny. "One . . . two—"

"Go!" I yelled.

"What about three?"

We burst from behind the fridge with a wild cry, dashing straight for the door. As we tore past the food prep island, something big stirred in the shadows to our left. Benny raised the can of Raid above his head and spritzed like he was writing the Declaration of Independence in the air.

Right away, my eyes stung. That sickly sweet chemical smell filled my nose.

"Watch where you're spraying!" I cried.

Something scuttled behind us. My overactive imagination pictured ten million cockroaches picking up speed. I risked a glance back.

It was worse.

The world's biggest praying mantis was charging straight at us, wearing a hungry expression and an apron that read: WHY YOU ALL UP IN MY GRILL?

Benny checked over his shoulder, and his eyes grew wider than a sumo wrestler's waistband. With a strangled scream, he poured on the speed.

From behind us came an unnatural cry that I swear sounded like, "Don't you dare leave that fridge door open!"

But I'm getting ahead of myself.

According to my teacher, Mr. Chu, you're supposed to grab your readers by the throat at the beginning of your story, but I feel like I'm just confusing you. You have no idea who Benny and I are, or why we're being chased through the kitchen by a giant bug.

And that's just not fair. (Both the confusion and the being chased, I mean.)

Let me back up a bit to where this story started. To the day Benny and I discovered what it really means to have a reputation as a monster fighter.

About the Author

Raised by wolves just outside Los Angeles, **BRUCE HALE** began his career as a writer while living in Tokyo, and continued it when he moved to Hawaii in 1983. Before entering the world of children's books, he worked as a magazine editor, toymaker, surveyor, corporate lackey, gardener, actor, and DJ.

From picture books to novels and graphic novels, Bruce has written and illustrated more than thirty-five books for kids, including his Chet Gecko Mysteries series, and his School for S.P.I.E.S. trilogy: *Playing with Fire*, *Thicker than Water*, and *Ends of the Earth*.

When not writing and illustrating, Bruce loves to perform. He has appeared onstage, on television, and in an independent movie called *The Ride*. Bruce is a popular speaker and storyteller for audiences of all ages. He has taught writing workshops at colleges and universities, and spoken at national conferences of writing, publishing, and literacy organizations. On top of that, Bruce has visited elementary schools across the country, from Hawaii, to Kansas, to Pennsylvania. (You'd never guess he loves to travel.)

These days, Bruce lives in Santa Barbara with his wife, Janette, and his sweet mutt, Riley. When he's not at the computer or drawing board, you'll find him hiking the hills, bicycling, or riding the waves (when it's warm enough, that is). He also likes going to movies and playing jazz music.